CHASE
through time

The Search for Grandpa Wally

CHASE
through time

The Search for Grandpa Wally

Jeff Vaala

INNER SUNSET MEDIA, LLC
SAN FRANCISCO, CA

ISBN: 978-1-6192712-0-3
Printed in the United States of America

Published by
Inner Sunset Media, LLC
1762 ½ 9th Ave
San Francisco, CA 94122
www.innersunsetmedia.com

Dedicated to Parents and Grandparents.

Pushing us forward...even if that's through scary doorways that lead to new adventures.

The unknown is scary.

The unknown is fun.

TEACHERS:

For the complementary Lesson Plans
and Class Presentation,
please visit www.chasethroughtime.com to download.

Passcode: GRANDPA

Acknowledgements

Kids and kids at heart can't be trapped when they possess the
willingness to move and an imagination. I think Chase, at the
beginning of the book, represents the side of ourselves that lets the
world dictate their life.

By the end of journey, he's changed, developed, grown.
The lowest pits can lead to greatest heights. This book
showed me that, one portal at a time.

This great publishing experiment also comes by way of an
amazing team of artists, designers, editors, readers and
advisors: Sarah, Eileen, Len, Mark, Toddy, Sue, Marcus,
Eric, Dan, Shannon and Kristin.

Several other people I'd like to thank as well.

My grandparents: With me even 20+ years
after they've passed.

My parents: Still with me to this day
and for that I'm grateful.

My friend Colby: a childhood friend and
trusted confidante to this day.

My target demographic, guinea pig reader,
sounding board and buddy: Max.

My partner in crime: Danielle.
Pushing me through another portal I didn't know
I wanted to take and grateful for her loving nudge.
She made me jump.
I am grateful for her love and affection.

TABLE OF CONTENTS

www.chasethroughtime.com

"When you let fear dictate the terms,
you'll always lose that negotiation.
When you attack fear, it doesn't seem so scary."

\- Grandpa Wally

Chapter 1

"I hate baloney!"

That was the only thing going through Chase Axelrod's mind as he snuck a peek into his backpack. His Mom had done it again. Baloney and cheese. On white bread. Dry and bland and rubbery. Lunch was gonna suck today!

A few hundred kids stormed past him on their way up the Upper West Side school's front steps. The 5-minute warning bell just finished its clangity-clang. But Chase wasn't focused on that. Nope, the twelve year-old New Yorker looked down again, yet nothing changed on the second peek. It was still a boring baloney sandwich. And from what he could tell, extra baloney. How could she have done this to him?! She knew. Heck, he told her all the time: "Anything but baloney!"

But at that moment, Chase's inner rage was interrupted. He looked up to see his sixth grade teacher…old lady Thatcher staring at him.

"Mr. Axelrod, let's save your sandwich for the lunch hour. Right now, you should be focused on history!" Chase trudged up the cold, concrete steps, through the littered hall and into Miss Thatcher's classroom.

Chase slung his backpack on his chair as Mrs. Thatcher bee-lined to the chalkboard. She quickly started the lesson.

"Blah, blah, blah…"

Chase tried to plug into the lecture but he was definitely behind. *Something about a man. Some guy named Marconi. Then something about Tesla. The radio…hmmm. I guess that's pretty cool.*

Chase tried. He really did. But she _was_ boring. She didn't even bring any examples. Like a real radio. One. Something. Anything. *C'mon, lady. Bring an example! Like an iPod. Or a Walkman. Or a picture of an iPod!* But she had nothing. No transistor. No car stereo. Nothing!

Chase attempted once more. He squinted. He leaned forward in his seat. He really, really tried to listen but all that came into his head was lunch…and how he missed breaking his high score on Super Mario Land on the ride to school. Those things and…*Man, she was boring!*

"Mr. Axelrod! Mr. Axelrod!"

Chase snapped out of his daydream.

"Mr. Axelrod, I didn't receive your homework. And before I get an imaginative reason why I didn't, please come to the board and fill in the answers to show you indeed did the reading."

Chase created a new definition for the word "slunk" as he rose from his seat. His body recoiled back, before swinging forward as he hoisted himself out of the old wooden chair. He shuffled slowly finally making it to the board. His snail's pace had a purpose. He was using this time to figure out the answers. Chase clearly spent the evening on his computer playing games and not reading the assigned lesson. He needed all the time his could muster. He slowly picked up the chalk and stepped back. He stared. And stared. And stared. Miss Thatcher cleared her throat. And she cleared it in that, "I'm getting annoyed" kind of way.

He stared at the chalkboard, three blanks needing to be answered:

Question One: *Radio is the transmission of signals by modulation of:*

A) Electromagnetic Waves

B) Microwaves

C) Gamma Rays

Question Two: *Before known as a "radio," this term was used to describe the transmission of sound waves?*

A) Wi-Fi

B) Wireless Telegraphy

C) Alternating Current

Question Three: *Who is responsible for inventing the radio?*

A) Tesla

B) Edison

C) Marconi

Chase quickly circled "A" on question one. First, his experience told him the answer to question one was always "A" with Miss Thatcher. (Plus, he knew the other two answers were just crazy.)

When it came to question two, he rightfully guessed "B" because again the other two answers were just crazy. Wi-Fi was a new term and alternating current has to do with the light socket, not the radio. That's how he reasoned and reasoned correctly.

Then it came to question number three. This one should be the easiest for him. This answer was more history than science. Not that he liked one better than the other, but he did fancy himself a boy who knew his history.

Chase wasn't a great student but he wasn't a dumb kid. Mostly straight C's. Nothing glamorous. Nothing Earth-shattering. Right down the middle. The kind of grades an unmotivated but fairly intelligent kid rightly deserved.

School *would* have come pretty easy to him if he just applied himself. But applying himself would mean more time in the textbooks and less time on the Nintendo DS. And that would entail him letting go of the quest for the high score and instead focusing on the highest grade. Ugh. *He was so close to solving each and every world on Super Mario!*

Of course, higher grades would also mean less hassle from his teachers and his parents. He could hear the nagging "advice" from Mom, Dad, Miss Thatcher and the rest: "you just need a little more application toward your homework and less time spent on the applications found on your iPod! Just a smidge more time and he would be a "B" student at least."

This would especially been the case in history. He loved history. Loved to read about it. Watch shows about it. Movies. Magazines. Museums. He loved history. LOVED IT!

Well, when someone else besides Mrs. Thatcher described it. She could suck the excitement out of the world's tallest roller coaster. So he didn't pay attention. And when you didn't pay attention in Mrs. Thatcher's class, you missed things. And when you missed things in class, you missed things on the exam. And that meant C's and D's and not the A's and B's that Chase could easily have gotten if he just paid attention. When his Mom or Dad would question him about it, he had one response and one response only: SHE'S BORING!

Then again, nothing compared to Chase's "real" history teacher: Grandpa Wally. Now Grandpa Wally could make anything in history sound awesome. He could take the most boring thing and describe it in great detail. Like he was there. Chase would love it. He could sit and listen for hours. And the best part was Grandpa Wally used props. Not real props but these real looking copies. He'd have things like gold coins from the Romans or a sword like the one used by King Arthur or a ring that could have been worn by Alexander the Great.

His Grandpa would talk about the way these great men would act or fight or eat or drink. He knew every little detail, every little fact. He knew more than the history books. Or maybe he knew every history book.

Chase always said, "Grandpa, you should be a history teacher." Grandpa would always smile and say that he was too old to teach a class. And he'd always tell Chase that the only student that mattered to him was Chase himself.

"I sure wish you'd drop that computer every now and then and pick up a book." Grandpa would sneak that line in when he came to visit. Not much, but every so often. Chase saw he wasn't trying to nag him. He saw his Grandfather wince immediately after the words escaped his mouth. But he also saw that it pained the elder man. Chase felt it so much that he actually would put the Gameboy down and peer over his Grandpa's shoulder at the book or encyclopedia he had opened. Chase didn't realize how much his Grandpa loved him. And how proud his grandfather became when he dropped the device and picked up the book. His grandpa loved it.

Speaking of love, there were three things Chase really loved…that weren't people: his Nintendo DSi with digital camera and music capabilities, his twenty-four Faber Castell Polychromos artist grade colored pencils and Hubba Bubba Max Original bubble gum.

Oh, he loved his mom…and his dad…and of course, Grandpa Wally and his dog Brooklyn and his skateboard and well, OK, he loved a lot of things but he really, really, really loved his Nintendo DSi, his markers and bubble gum.

And there was one thing he really hated….BALONEY!

Why couldn't he get that out of his head? *Baloney!*

He stared at question three and the answers sat there in front of him and all that popped into his head was the word baloney.

"Mr. Axelrod, care to make a guess?"

Chase looked away from the board and back to Miss Thatcher.

"Because you obviously don't know the answer…"

It finally hit him…*oh yeah, Marconi! The radio! Italian guy.*

Chase circled answer "C." Then he confidently put the chalk down on the small ledge. He took a step back…at the same moment Miss Thatcher took a step forward. "I'm sorry, Mr. Axelrod but the correct answer was 'A.' Nikola Tesla invented the radio.

The class giggled. Chase went red and his heart sank to his shoes.

"Obviously class, it pays to read your assignments and come to school prepared or else you look like a fool while standing in front of the class. Chase wanted to crawl under a rock and hide. And he probably would have but: RRRIIIINNNNNNGGGGGGGGGGGG!!!!!!!!!!

The class bell! The only thing that could get Mrs. Thatcher to stop embarrassing him and the class to pop out of their seats like rockets firing into the sky. Everyone ran…except Chase. He knew he was about to get lectured. And this time alone.

"Mr. Axelrod, you need to change your actions. You are smarter than this. You have all the ability in the world—"

Chase cut her off. "I really think that answer is wrong. The right answer is Marconi."

"Mr. Axelrod, now is not the time! We are not talking about one answer right now but rather your overall performance."

"But--!"

"--Mr. Axelrod! This is not a debate. This is a warning. Improve your attitude and improve your grades, or you will be repeating this grade over next year. Am I clear?"

Chase eked out the word: "ok."

What he wanted to say was: "if the answer to question three was correct, you couldn't yell at me because I would have been three for three." But he couldn't say that right now. Even though, he believed he was right, there was no arguing with Miss Thatcher. He just stood silently, waiting for her to dismiss him.

"It is time for lunch. Why don't you run along?"

Chase turned to leave when another horrible thought hit him. *Lunch....ugh: Baloney!*

Well today, even baloney sounded better than Mrs. Thatcher. Chase snatched his backpack and hustled out the door. As he did, a devious grin formed on his face. It was time to do some trading. There had to be someone in the lunchroom who would fall for...er, I mean, enjoy the pleasurable opportunity of eating a double baloney and cheese sandwich. Yup, Chase had to get his game on. He needed to find someone gullible.

Then he rounded the corner: BINGO!

There stood his first choice...waiting in the hot lunch line. If he could have found anybody in the entire school, it would be none other than, Farley Cudman. A smile appeared on his face. Chase sets his sights on Farley and moved in. Time to make a deal!

"Hey Farley, hungry today?"

This question never needed to be asked. Farley was always hungry. Always! You wouldn't know it by looking at him. Farley was five inches taller than any person in sixth grade and as skinny as a flagpole but he never, ever stopped eating. He never stopped eating and he never stopped growing. Weeds were jealous of how fast he grew. But he never looked like he gained weight, just height.

No matter, today Chase's goal wasn't to break down the growing patterns of Farley Cudman, just get him to change his lunch plans.

"Wanna trade?"

"Whatcha got?"

"A sandwich...extra meat."

"Extra?"

"Twice as big as usual. A real gut-filler."

"Turkey?"

"Nope. Better."

"Better?"

"Better. Beef."

"Roast Beef?"

"It's not roasted. It's just beef based."

"Beef based?"

"Yeah, made from beef."

"What is it?"

"It's beef and cheese on white bread."

"Any mayo?"

"Nope."

"Good."

"Just mustard."

"Mustard?"

"On the side. Mustard packets. In case you like that."

"I like mustard."

"Yeah, so do I. So you want to trade?"

Farley squished his mouth together. That meant Farley was thinking. With Farley, it always started with his mouth. The way Farley's lips moved and smushed and opened and closed, it actually looked like he was imagining the sandwich. Like he was eating it first. Letting it hit his taste buds and tasting every single bite.

Chase started to wonder if his sandwich even existed anymore. He had to peek back into the brown bag to make sure Farley hadn't magically pulled it out and somehow was eating it. When he checked, it was still there. Still untouched. Still Baloney.

"Baloney!"

Chase's head shot up. "uh-oh" he thought.

"You said it was beef! But that's Baloney!"

"Yeah, but it's baloney...*made from beef!* It's the best baloney out there."

"You were trying to trick me!"

"Swear it on the sun, Farley. Swear it true. I was not trying to trick you. I'd never do that to you. We're friends. And friends don't do that to other friends."

"So if we're friends, why'd you ask me today?"

"What do you mean?"

"Today is Dunker Day."

Oh no! Chase didn't know that. It was Dunker Day. Italian Dunker Day. That was a holiday. Or should be.

Except that if it were a holiday, there would be no school and then there'd be no dunkers. So, to the kids of Thomas Alva Edison Middle School, Dunker Day was an "In-School" holiday. And the face of Chase Axelrod fell flat to the floor. There was no way any trade was going to happen today. No one in their right mind would be trading Dunkers for a baloney and cheese sandwich. No matter how much extra meat was piled on that sandwich.

Chase slunk back to his normal table. His buddies were already powering down their dunkers. Garlic cheese bread and marinara sauce. Three slices of French bread piled high with cheese and melted into a gooey good combination. It looked like the meal they served kings and queens. And at the moment, Chase was no king. Just a fool…with an extra big baloney and cheese sandwich.

Lunch could not end any faster. Watching those guys savor their dunkers while he ate his crummy sandwich was not making this day a good day. He had rummaged through the bottom of his backpack for loose change only to come up 75¢ short. And "his boys" had nothing to offer in support. His buddy, Max had exactly the correct amount for dunkers and his other buddy Jaxson was a nickel short. A nickel short didn't faze the lunch lady. She let him pass.

"Just bring it tomorrow."

Seventy-five cents, however, was not excusable. No how, no way! Even with all the charm Chase could muster. A smile. A sheepish look. A promise to bring it tomorrow. None of it worked.

"If I let seventy-five cents pass for you, I'd have to let it pass for everyone. And I just can't return the cash drawer that short. Sorry, son. You're just going to have to eat your baloney sandwich." Chase slugged back to his seat, unwrapped his sandwich and choked it down.

One bite in, he saw Alex, the cute blond girl that sat next to him in history class. He thought about asking her...but then thought again. She'd just witnessed his public embarrassment at the hands of Miss Thatcher. He didn't need any more humiliation today. Plus, when it was all said and done, he wasn't a big fan of girls in the first place.

The end of lunch meant the beginning of free time. In this middle school, students didn't go out and play kickball or tag like they did in that kiddy school he used to go to. No, here at Edison Middle, it meant time to play with his DS. That was the only reason he ate that baloney sandwich...to get excused from lunch and back to his Super Mario game.

The other kids played games and chatted. They laughed and joked and teased and gossiped. Chase didn't. He just played DS. His friends...well, the two that he ate near, they did the same thing. All of them, heads down and noses in their games. They never said a word. All that was heard was the clicking of buttons and the occasional sigh of frustration when their guy died. It was the quietest section in the entire lunchroom.

This lunch hour produced its second disappointment. When he reached into his backpack, he noticed the Super Mario Land game wasn't in the DS. Chase frantically searched his bag, turning it inside out. No game. No Super Mario. And he had paused it at such a crucial point. He was about to solve the entire game. He was so close this morning but then his mother told him he had to hustle. He was late for school. Agghh!

And now the entire game was missing. This lunch hour was going to suck! In fact, when he went through all the pockets, the only game he could find was an old game his Grandpa had mailed him a few months ago. The Battle for Athens. He'd never heard of it before he opened the package. The one time he popped it in, it seemed like a history game rather than a single shooter or adventure game and it was quickly removed.

Grandpa is good at a lot of things but he probably shouldn't dabble in buying games for the DS. But Chase had fifteen minutes to kill and no other options. Guess this would do.

When it booted up, he had two choices: Peloponnesian War or Corinthian War. Never heard of either but he chose the latter. As he tried to comprehend the strategy, he noticed a lot of familiar words. In fact, it started to interest him and was as the perfect lead into next period.

Once lunch was over, Chase always got excited. To him, the real fun of school began. Right after lunch was Chase's favorite class: Latin and Greek. It was really an advanced language class that showed the huge influence of these two languages on present day English. How all the words we use today when we speak or write all descended from these two old, archaic languages. Language, Chase learned, was like a puzzle and words could be broken down into parts. And he had seen some of these words in The Battle for Athens game. As class started, he couldn't help but think that new game might be a little cooler than he thought.

Miss Baker's Latin and Greek class that taught him where the "opolis" at the end of cities like Minneapolis or Indianapolis actually meant "city" in Greek. He also learned where we got words like "*music*" and "*theory*" and "*acne*" and "*geometry*" and "*cycle*" and "*guitar*" and "*logic*" and even "*history.*" They all came from the Greek language.

And from Latin, we get words like "*alien*" and "*marine*" and "*sinister*" and "*action*" and "*video*" and "*revolution*" and "*pugnacious*" and "*compute*" and "*science.*"

At school, Chase just sort of blended into the situation. Whether that was at class, or in the halls or on the athletic field, Chase was just there. Not someone who called attention to himself. He really would be considered a social chameleon. He fit into situations but he didn't stand out. No one noticed him being out of place but then again, no one really noticed him.

He had some other "friends…" Besides the guys at the lunch table. Kids he knew. Kinda talked to. Played vids with. He wasn't real social but for a "gamer," Chase wasn't a bad athlete. Not real active but not a slouch.

Chase got along with most people but he wasn't going to win class president any time soon. He was ok with that. Besides, that didn't matter at the moment, right now all that mattered was Latin and Greek and that the minutes of the hour were ticking by too fast.

It always did. He loved the class and he loved <u>this</u> teacher. Mrs. Baker. The coolest lady at Edison Middle. She and Grandpa Wally had a lot in common. They loved to talk but not in that "I'm so much smarter than you and you should realize it" way. No, she just started talking and kids would just start listening. It was almost like they were zombies or something. And Chase was at the lead. At the moment, he was so excited. So much so he was doing his homework for the next week. And almost finished.

He was deep in the lesson…which is why he didn't quite realize when the whole class was staring at him. He looked up. Every kid's eyeballs focused on him. He looked back toward the chalkboard and Mrs. Baker was speaking to him. His heart started pounding. His palms sweaty. *Not again. Not today!*

"Chase? Your mother…" He followed her eyes. To the classroom door. And there stood his Mom. Chase sat stunned. He didn't move. He certainly didn't speak. He was hardly processing.

"Chase, come on, we have to go."

Chase was that zombie right now. He slowly got up—

"—grab all your stuff. C'mon, we have to get going. We're meeting your Dad."

Chase finally kicked it into gear, grabbing his backpack and papers and the lesson. By the time he looked back to his mom, she was gone. Down the hallway.

His mom was walking really fast. So fast that Chase had to run to catch up. And just as he did, her hand extended and shoved a plastic grocery bag into his chest.

"Here, put these in your backpack." She handed him his pencils. And several packages of bubble gum.

"I couldn't find your DS."

"It's in my backpack."

"Good. Cause we're not going home."

"Where are we going?"

"To the airport."

"Why?"

"Cause we're flying to Minneapolis."

"Why?"

She was quiet. Deep in thought. So was Chase. There was only one reason he could think of going to Minneapolis. Grandpa Wally lived there. Well, he lived two hours outside of Minneapolis. And that's the only reason they ever flew from New York to Minneapolis.

"Are we going to see Grandpa?"

His mother nodded…then stopped, "Well, I hope so."

"What do you mean?" She was back in thought. And walking faster. They were cruising through the school. "Mom, what do you mean?"

She stopped at the front doors and turned around. Her face had the most serious look Chase had ever seen.

"About your Grandpa…"

Her voice trailed off. She composed herself and continued, "He's gone."

Chase had to think about that. *Gone?! What does she mean, gone?* Then he thought he got it, "Gone, like dead?"

His mother quickly replied, "NO." Then she thought. "Well, we don't know. He may have wandered off. So I can't say whether he's gone or *gone*."

A rush of horrible feelings shot through Chase's brain. *Not Grandpa Wally. No! Not him. It just can't be. I hadn't seen him since summer and we just talked on the phone last week but…he can't be gone!*

His Mom kept talking and Chase finally snapped back from his horrible scenario to hear her go on, "I just can't say, Chase. I just can't say. But they think he's still alive. They think."

"Who? Who thinks that?"

"The sheriff. The sheriff thinks he's somewhere."

Chapter 2

"Where's Grandpa?"

While the plane ride seemed quick, the car ride felt a lot longer than normal. And the answer to Chase's question still wasn't answered. It wasn't answered at school. It wasn't answered in the airport. On the flight. Or in the two-hour car ride either. The only clue he ever saw was the occasional tear escaping his mother's eye. And she quickly wiped that away before it would dare drop down her cheek.

In between tears, she might clear a sniffle. Chase's Dad kept one hand on the steering wheel and the other clutched his wife's hand. This was serious and Chase knew it. The car ride was quiet. Quiet and sad.

Nothing to do but sit back and wait until they arrived. Chase dug into his backpack for his DS. Maybe it would make the time fly by until they arrived at their destination.

It sat on the hill, the highest hill in the county, looking lonely and decrepit. Like it was mourning. The farmhouse stood atop the horizon like it always had for the past hundred years. The largest house in the county, it was revered for its majesty. Ornate windows and doors plus an enormous front porch, where Chase used to spend summers listening to Grandpa spin tales of the Romans and Visigoths, Trojans and Spartans, the Normans and the Saxons. It was the location of so many great memories. The excitement of rounding the highway and creeping up the last hill near a grove of oaks and pines, the spires of the house would pierce the sky. A few more seconds and the entire house would come into view. It was an inviting sight for Chase and his family. Well, usually. Today though, it wasn't the place they wished they were heading.

This was the farmhouse where his mother grew up, he had heard the story a million times, but he'd never thought of it as Mom's home. Nope. It was Grandpa Wally's. And right now, the tallest farmhouse in Tinkerton County looked sad.

Chase and his parents came over the hill to see a police car on the long, dirt driveway. Actually there were two sheriff cars and a few pick-ups. All dirty and all lined up as though a parade was about to begin…or maybe a funeral. There wasn't a hearse. At least, Chase couldn't see one.

The sheriff met his parents at the porch steps and wasted no time in bringing them up to speed. He was holding a map of the county, a map that had been dissected with various color patterns like it was a cheap imitation for a coloring book. As Chase squeezed into their tight circle, through the gaps in their bodies, he thought he could see the colored shapes were actually zones for the search party. Most of the blue and purple zones had been covered in the past twenty-four hours but that's because they were much flatter.

"Primarily corn and wheat fields. We got through those by midday. Now, the red, green, yellow and orange…well, as you may know Ma'am, those all run along Caribou Creek. And they are much hillier."

The Sheriff went on to explain the little "nooks and crannies" that formed along the crooked, winding creek. "It's rocky and it's slick…and well, we've had a lot of rain fall this spring. Add that to all the snowmelt and if someone were to accidentally slip on the rocks and get caught in the current, well…"

Chase's mom stifled another sniffle. In her head, she played out the worst-case scenario that was possible.

"If he did fall into—"

The sheriff cut her off immediately, "—we don't think he fell into the creek, we're just making sure. The creek has been dragged and authorities downstream have been notified of the missing person. If he had slipped and fell…well, by now someone in Rochester or Marquette counties would have spotted a body."

His mother was silent. Chase could tell she didn't like when the sheriff said the word, "body." It was like he was already saying Grandpa Wally was dead. The sheriff caught her eye...and her snarly look and rapidly added, "and no one has found a body...which gives us hope."

Chase had tired with all the talk of logistics and search parties. When he had conjured up a question, he was roundly ignored and pushed back from the inner circle. "Fine, I'll go someplace else," he softly uttered. Defiant as he was, no one heard him whisper it. And no one saw him wander inside.

Cluttered. Dark and cluttered. That would be the best word to describe Grandpa Wally's house. Books, papers, furniture and lots and lots of things: mementos and pictures, clothes, hats, photo albums, knick-knacks, oh and dust. Lots and lots of dust. Grandpa Wally was never one to worry about the dust. Not since Grandma Lucy passed away and stopped asking him to clean up after himself. Nope. The dust stayed. And grew...thick. Thick as the stacks of books next to Grandpa's old armchair. Chase had to sit in it. He was compelled.

Chase removed his backpack, dropping it at his feet as he sat down. He immediately felt closer to his Grandpa. The arms worn by years of elbows rubbing them to a shiny fabric gloss. The top of the chair just a shade darker from the hair tonic Grandpa rubbed into his hair every morning. And the entire chair smelled. It smelled of musty knowledge and achy ointment cream. In short, to Chase, it smelled like Grandpa Wally. Normally, that would be considered a little stinky to his nose. But now, with these circumstances, the odor was a pretty cool reminder of his favorite person.

Chase sat still, but his eyes darted around the room. He was pretending he was sitting on Grandpa Wally's lap. Like he did as a kid. His mind began to drift…he could hear his Grandpa talking:

"It was a summer day on the beaches of Vera Cruz. Really early in the morning. The fresh smell of flowers drowned out by the sea salt in the air, wafting up from the Gulf of Mexico. The sun barely reaching the horizon but that wasn't the light that scared the men of Hernando Cortes' fleet. No, the light that scared them was the sight of every ship in the fleet burning like torches climbing toward the sky. Their ships were burning! The very ships that would allow them to escape the treacherous countryside filled with angry Aztecs, ready to defend their homeland. The same Aztecs who had successfully defended this land for centuries. And the same Aztecs who had fought off every single attack and attempt to be conquered by European explorers.

Any hope for escape was eliminated. Cortes was going to accomplish his goals no matter the consequences. But he needed his men to be committed. So he had his fleet of eleven boats lit on fire. There was no going back. He and 600 soldiers marched on Tenochtitlan, then the main city of Mexico and home to Montezuma, leader of the Aztecs. Cortes conquered the city six months later. Without a way back, there was no way to go but forward. They burned the boats."

Snapping out of his memory, Chase looked over at the small end table that held the latest books and papers. Wedged into a crack of book stacks was a tiny pewter Clipper ship. Maybe this was like one of Cortes' ships. Maybe not. Chase held onto it, slipping it into his pocket.

The miniature ship wasn't just a reminder of his grandfather, it also triggered him to stand up and hustle to the back of the house, backpack in hand. Just off of the kitchen, a rickety door led down to the basement and many more treasures.

The basement of the house looked more like a catacomb than the structure that supported this old house on its high hill perch. Musty and damp, the ceilings hung low, the cracked cement floor held a layer of earth that made one wonder if any concrete existed beneath it and the walls looked like they were about to cave in. Thank goodness for the boxes that stretched to the rafters. They were probably the main force holding the walls upright.

Chase stopped to survey the entire setting. The basement rooms seemed to be smaller than last summer. Maybe they were. Then again, maybe Grandpa just found more stuff at the garage sales and flea markets he must have attended.

This spot was a familiar spot for Chase. He loved the treasures that existed down here. His Grandpa would tell him to open a box and pick something out. Anything. A sword. A hat. A map. Anything that caught his eye. And anything he picked out would have a story with it. For the next twenty minutes, Grandpa would talk about the day he found this treasure. He would describe it uses and its value. He would describe where he found it. Who gave it to him. Why he grabbed it.

Then they'd work their way through the room, opening more boxes finding more mementos and the stories attached to them. When Chase was young, he believed his Grandpa's stories. Now that he was older, he'd smile outwardly and laugh on the inside. Grandpa sure could tell some big tales. The biggest, actually. But Chase didn't care. They were entertaining and he let Grandpa just keep talking.

In the next room, much smaller than the first, there would be two or three trunks. Old steamer trunks that looked like they had traveled on the Titanic or some similar ship. Some useful storage on passage from London to New York, carrying furs and jewels for the aristocrats of the day. The edges of the trunks were worn. The side beaten by their carriers. The clasp and lock a little worse for wear. But inside…boy inside, they were filled with gifts.

Anytime Chase would visit, he could pull some treasure of his liking and take it upstairs. This would mean an evening on the porch with Grandpa and the fireflies. It would mean stories that would never end until Chase's eyelids grew too heavy for the day. And it would always end with Grandpa snapping the sleepy Chase back to consciousness and the offer that if he wanted to, he could keep the little treasure for himself.

Back at the trunk, Chase dropped his backpack to the side before he opened the creaky container. As he did, there was his favorite sight in the world: one of Grandpa Wally's cigar boxes. The same cigar boxes that he would receive every September on his birthday. The same type of cigar box that held his toy airplanes, pencils, medals, Civil War bullets, carved limestone figures, cards, souvenirs…all the little things that little boys love.

As Chase looked down into the trunk, one thing caught his attention, another cigar box, wrapped in no less than twenty rubber bands. Big rubber bands. The industrial kind. Wrapped around two, sometimes three times. And on a cigar box that contained one word written on top of it. The word: CHASE.

His eyes exploded open. "Grandpa already has my birthday gift! COOL!" He reached to grab it when…

"CHASE!!!" A hand had come down on top of his shoulder causing Chase to jump a foot in the air.

"Yikes!" Chase was scared to death at the volume. He turned to see his Dad standing there.

"Chase! I've been looking for you for ten minutes! Get up here! There's somebody who'd like to meet you."

The young boy slowly rose and walked toward his Dad.

"Don't wander off like that! We don't need anybody else lost!"

As the two walked toward the stairs, Chase slowed to glance to his left. The opposite side of the stairs. Where the light never seems to creep. The dark corner of the basement. The section that he'd never seen. The section he'd never been brave enough to explore. He thought about that. *Why haven't I ever been in that room? Maybe because light doesn't seem to get back there. And it's totally scary in this basement without light.*

In the past, he'd always just turned right at the end of the steps and headed straight for the trunks. In this moment, though, for some strange reason, he was drawn to look a little deeper. He even leaned forward. Took a few steps toward it, squinting to get a better look but to no avail. It was just too dark to see anything.

"CHASE! C'mon!"

When they reached the kitchen, there sat Aunt Ethel. Old, rotund Aunt Ethel. As big as a refrigerator. And very huggy. Too huggy. Way too huggy!

After Chase pried himself from her death grip of a hug, and wiped the wet kiss from his cheek, he made sure the table always separated them from each other.

"Chase, did your mother start making this spaghetti?"

Chase had no idea what she was talking about.

"This spaghetti and meat sauce. On the stove. Was that your mother's doing?"

Chase could only shrug.

"Chase, cat got your tongue? Did someone leave this?"

"Nope. That was Mr. Franklin's. He left that on the stove." The sheriff had entered the room with Chase's mom. "This was exactly how the house was found. We think he must have wandered off in the middle of making dinner."

Aunt Ethel dabbed her finger into the saucepan. She took a taste, making a face in the process, "Well, I guess that's not bad Bolognese for three days old."

After dinner, Chase sat on the front porch. His mind wandered from the many memories of Grandpa Wally. The adults yammered on inside about search plans and rescue strategies. They wondered aloud how long he had been suffering from dementia. They wondered why he never mentioned anything. They all took blame for not being more supportive and attentive and more present. Then they all consoled each other. *There was no way they could have known. Every one gets old. You can't stop it.* And as they kept on talking in circles, Chase kept thinking about the good things while the rest had the bad things covered.

The creaky screen door interrupted his thoughts. It was his dad again. His entrance wasn't like this afternoon, when he scared the tar out of Chase. This time he was slower, softer and more mellow.

"How you doing, Buddy?"

"Fine."

His dad sat down on the other chair. "Things are a little crazy for you, huh?"

"I'm fine."

"Yeah?"

"Yeah."

The two Axelrod men sat quietly for a few minutes until his Dad spoke again, "It's OK if you're not."

This caused Chase to stare at his Dad.

"I know you loved Grandpa Wally. He was a great man."

"Is he dead?"

"What?! No." His dad quickly corrected.

"You said 'was.'"

"I'm sorry. I didn't mean that." His dad looked like he had more to say so Chase just sat still.

"Son, sometimes grandpas go away. We all go away sometime."

"But you just said he didn't die."

"Well, we don't know."

"So he could be around. Like in the next town over."

"They've checked the next town over, Buddy. And the next one after that."

"But they haven't checked the next one over from that, have they? Or the next one after that?"

His dad got it. He saw the hope his son had. And he couldn't say for certain about the search so he didn't. "Nope. I guess they haven't. Let's hope he's in the next town over. Or over. Or over. Let's go to bed thinking he's out there somewhere, ok?"

Chase nodded. His dad agreed. They headed inside.

From the kitchen window, Chase could see down the hill, where Grandpa's barn sat next to the horse pasture and the tractor shed. And leaning on the rails of the horse pasture was Chase's mom. He slipped through the back screen door and ventured down the back hill toward his mother.

They both stood silent for a while. She was deep in thought. Chase let her stay in that world for a few minutes.

"Mom, did you like growing up here?"

His mom shook her head. When she turned slightly toward Chase, he saw she'd been crying a little.

"I just talked to Dad. We figure he's like four towns over. Maybe five."

His mom said nothing but gave Chase the biggest hug she'd ever given. It was almost as smothering as Aunt Ethel's hug except his Mom was a 150 pounds smaller and didn't smell like mothballs. And it felt a whole lot better. Except it went on a little longer than her usual hugs.

"What I'd give to just hug your grandpa one more time."

Chase wanted to break the hug until that moment. Then he figured she needed a little more hugging and since Grandpa Wally wasn't there, he'd better step in and step up.

Mom and son were making their way back to the house up the long sloped hill when Chase noticed two huge steel doors right in the middle of their incline. These doors looked like they were heading straight into the ground. A set of doors right into the hillside.

The doors were rusted over and almost invisible unless you were right on top of them. The grass and the weeds had done their best to hide it from view and with the brown rust color: the doors just seemed to be a patch of dirt in the middle of a huge lawn. Chase had never noticed them before in all his visits to Grandpa's house. And here he thought he had seen everything on that hill.

"Mom, what are these for?"

"Tornados and Russians."

Chase looked puzzled at her answer.

"It's called a fallout shelter. Back in the 50's…well, I guess from the fifties all the way until the eighties, we all worried the Russians would drop the bomb on us. These would lead to a deep room where we could go if the sirens went off. Your grandpa's father built it before I was born."

"Grandpa had a dad?"

"Yes, silly. Grandpa had a dad. He was your great-grandfather."

"And he lived here?"

"Yes, he built this house…and this shelter."

"Why?"

"At first, in case of a tornado. But he made it bigger and stronger and deeper because he was scared of the Russians."

"Huh?"

"It was supposed to be safe. Where we could live if the whole world blew up."

"Blew up?"

"Yeah. Blew up. The fear was the Russians were going to kill us all."

"And you were going to live in a cave?"

"Sort of. More like a fort. It was supplied with canned food and beds and a little place where we could survive."

"Have you ever been inside it?"

"Once, when I was little, but your Grandpa locked it up and told us the Russians weren't ever going to bomb so we didn't really need it."

Chase tried the door but it didn't budge. Not even a little. The lock on the flap was rusted shut.

His mom noticed the lock too, "You'd need a welder to get that open."

Chase could only agree after he pulled with all his might unsuccessfully.

"I think you can access it from the basement. I think...I don't remember. Of course maybe your grandfather closed that off too."

Chase stared at it. And it stared back. Like a challenge. *Bet you'll never see inside me.*

"C'mon Chase, it's time for bed. We have a big day tomorrow. We're not going to sit around here all day. We're going to help search for Grandpa."

Chase finally broke his curious stare at the secret doorway that led to the mysterious shelter existing under Grandpa's house.

"What did you say earlier, five towns over?"

Chase nodded.

Grandpa Wally called it "Chase's Room." Because he reckoned, Chase was the only person to sleep in it in the last twenty years and probably would be the only whoever would. On the dresser, some of the old toys sat in formation. Chase had army men from years past and an old baseball. He had broken pencils that he had left behind and a few old sketches he had left for Grandpa. But they were still sitting where he had left them so he guessed Grandpa didn't want them.

Chase studied up a few of them. Paging through the drawings, he saw the one where he drew the tractor in the barn. He drew one of the Big Oak in the front yard, complete with tire swing. He drew one of his grandpa on the front porch as he sat under that Big Oak. Then the last one. The view from his bedroom window. He didn't remember drawing that one. Wait! Yes he did. It was the afternoon that Grandpa wasn't feeling well and spent the day napping. It was raining outside so Chase perched himself in the bedroom window, looking at the wet farm world. He decided to draw the landscape. He looked at the drawing again. The barn. The horses in the pasture. The cows grazing. The shed. The fence. The picnic table. The grassy hill. The dirt path leading down to the barn. The view of it all.

As he looked at it, he was happy…and proud of himself. I did a pretty good job on that one he thought. He set the sketches back on the dresser and fell into bed. Still in his clothes, he was asleep in seconds.

Chapter 3

"Something's in the Basement!"

Chase's eyes popped open. Right out of a dead sleep. *That's it! It was in the sketch!*

He jumped out of bed, clicking on the light before grabbing the sketch of the backyard. Studying it intently, his eyes scanned the pencil strokes.

There it is! The sketch had the fallout shelter in it. He <u>had</u> seen it before. But he had forgotten it. *Why?! Why didn't he remember it?!* Try as he might, he couldn't wrap his brain around it. But try as he might, he couldn't get another thought out of his brain. Those doors led somewhere. There was something behind them. What if it was Grandpa!? What if he was trapped inside?! What if he wasn't five towns over but three stories below? Maybe he had wandered down there and was hurt and couldn't move or yell or talk or…Chase knew what he had to do. He had to get a closer look. He had to act!

His bedroom door slowly opened. Just a crack…and enough for his eyes to look across the hallway at the room in which his parents were supposed to be sleeping. The door was shut. The coast was clear.

Chase took very slow and cautious steps as he snuck from his bedroom. The floor was creaky. But that made sense because the house was rickety. It sounded like bones cracking with every step. Especially in the middle of the night.

Chase needed to be careful. He knew his parents would have scolded him for being up so late. It was well past midnight. He knew they'd march him right back to bed. He knew they'd guilt him to lie back down because tomorrow was going to be long and tiring. Of course, he'd tell them he was young and had the energy and he'd be fine and they shouldn't worry so much but he also knew they'd never accept his argument. So instead, he must be careful and sneak down the steps.

The steps stood twenty feet away. He had been extremely quiet for the first ten feet but now the tricky part remained. The next ten feet passed directly in front of his parent's bedroom. And once he got past their door, he had to tip toe down the even creakier stairs that ran along the other wall of that same bedroom until they dropped far enough down to the first floor. Chase stood still, looking at the gauntlet that lay before him and measuring the amount of skill this would take.

It was at this peaceful moment that the silence was broken…by crying. Muffled through the door, he could tell those were the same tearful sounds he had heard near the horse pasture. His heart fell. *This was killing Mom. And there was nothing she could do. Until tomorrow. Then she'd do what she could. And Chase would help all he could but he's just a kid and they didn't really expect that much from him. They couldn't, could they?* Besides, he was going to try and help out right now. He was going to explore the basement. *Maybe the answer lay right below them!*

Chase's thoughts were interrupted by louder sniffles. He also heard his dad say something he couldn't make out. But Dad was there. He was comforting. He had things under control. Chase had a fallout shelter to explore. And he also had his diversion. They wouldn't hear him if he moved quick and quiet. Quick and quiet. Quick and quiet.

Before Chase knew it, he was half way down the stairs and on the first floor. Clear. Quick and quiet...and successful. Explorer Chase Axelrod had conquered his first hurdle. *This just might to be fun!*

Moments later, when he was outside...unsuccessfully tugging on the locked shelter doors, his mind changed. Ten minutes after that, when he stood at the top of the steps leading down to the basement, fun wasn't even close to the word he would describe the moment.

Twenty more minutes later, he stared at the dark corner of the basement. The place where the sun never shined. The place where light refused to go. Chase had another "F" word in mind. "FEAR!" But he had to go forward. He knew he had to...Grandpa could be trapped. He held that thought in his head. In his hand, he held a tiny little flashlight. The beam barely worked.

It looked like it might die at any moment. The light flickered, struggling to cut through the darkness. And he kept looking down at it, as though it would provide bravery and courage and maybe, just maybe the guts to take a step forward.

See, before Chase had found himself staring at the black abyss that lived under Grandpa Wally's house, Chase had taken his usual right hand turn at the bottom of the steps. He passed by the mountains of boxes. His goal was certain. He was headed for the trunks. The trunks that held his cigar box or at least the cigar box that had his name on it. He had to know what was inside. If Grandpa never came back, he would have never known what was inside. And that would be a shame. He knew his birthday was six months away but Grandpa wasn't there. And may never, ever be again so he could easily justify opening it. Plus, it might have a clue inside.

As he opened the trunk, the cigar box wasn't the only thing he found. He also discovered his backpack. He had forgotten it there this afternoon when his dad snuck up on him. Making him go upstairs to meet Aunt Ethel and get those never ending hugs and that sloppy forehead kiss. A miserable moment. But then again, well, she did make a pretty good spaghetti and meat sauce. So good, that Chase actually had a second helping. Boy, Farley would have eaten three plates…maybe four! If Farley had a Great Aunt Ethel, he may actually gain weight….maybe.

But enough about Farley, Chase thought. *What's in that box?* Chase pulled it out and began his examination. Before he opened it, and pulled off the fifteen or so rubber bands that sealed the flip top box, he carefully eyed the outside. On top, his name made by black marker and in the familiar handwriting of Grandpa Wally. The yellow King Edward label. Slightly peeling from the corner edges. The sides of the box were pretty scraped up, kind of like the trunk in which it laid. From what Chase could figure, this box had been used before. No matter. The box didn't matter as much as the contents.

Rubber band after rubber band hit the floor. They seemed to be wrapped in a cross over method making Chase have to turn the box back and forth as each layer was removed.

Finally, he worked the last band off the top edge. And then the bottom edge. It snapped back on Chase's fingers. OUCH! The rubber band whistled across the room, hitting the back wall. The cigar box fell to the concrete floor. CRASH!

Chase's eyes were big as saucers. Did something break?! With the mound of rubber bands on the floor and the floor covered in that long generated layer of dirt, Chase dropped to one knee and discovered that nothing was broken…not that the contents of the box weren't in a million pieces. But that's what the box held. A lot of little things.

"That's funny?!" Chase thought. *Usually Grandpa gives me a souvenir from one of his trips and it's only one big thing. And it's cool. And it's something I don't have. Which is really cool. He's never dropped a bunch of trinkets in a box and passed it off as a gift.* But this time he had.

When Chase collected all the little things, he started to examine the contents.

- A Sharpie marker. Probably the same one that was used to write his name on the box top.

- Lemon Drops and Butter Rum Life Savers. These used to be Grandma's favorite before she died. Chase never liked them that much, but whatever.
- Paper clips. Like fifty of them. And all different sizes.
- A small buck knife. Ok, that's pretty cool. It looks old and used. The blade took a little effort to open but once it did, it was six inches long and looked really sharp. Boy, Mom would never let me keep this.
- A large rubber band. Another one? Guess so. But this one is bigger than he's ever seen. It's about a foot in length. Chase tried to stretch it and he could almost pull it from outstretched hand to outstretched hand.
- Four old looking keys. The kind that wouldn't work today. No, these looked like they would open a castle door or a dungeon. Or the lock of a paddock or a guillotine or a…well, it would open some old doors.
- A magnifying glass. About three or four inches across the glass. Oh, the ants he could have burned when he was younger.
- A compass.
- Some blank sheets of paper.
- A tiny pen light.
- A miniature sewing kit.
- Two double AA batteries.
- Three yards of string. Or cord. Like tiny mountain climber cord but only as big and thick as string.

Stuck to the bottom of the box was a small leather book. Well, more like a pamphlet. But it was blue leather. And imprinted on the cover was a picture of the sun.

A sun with many rays coming out of the middle. Sixteen to be exact.

Chase quickly counted.

The rays alternated. One squiggly and one straight. All the way around the center of the sun. On the center of the sun was a face. A kind of sinister face. Partially smiling, partially frowning. And altogether creepy looking.

When Chase opened the book, all it contained on the first page was codes. Or what looked like codes.

More pictures of suns. Some different symbols. A few math equations. Some lines written in different languages. Maybe translations, thought Chase.

On the next page, a few weird poems and on the last page, a set of rules.

The Rules
(They read as such):

The world you affect can only be the one in which you were born. (Like a good camper, leave only footprints, take only memories)

The tallest building or structure is the way out.

The sun will always guide you.

You've been given more gifts than you need. Use them. And use them wisely.

With every step in life comes a little more education.
Learn from them.

Adventure is a forward activity. There is no going back.

Fear is natural, paralysis from it, is not.

Becoming a man is scary, but necessary.
You must decide when you're ready.

As Chase finished reading the rules, he discovered another piece of paper stuck in the box. It was a note from Grandpa:

I'm fighting Alexander the Great or building a pyramid in Giza or maybe I've found a real magic carpet and am on the ride of my life. I may be running four minutes with Bannister or ascending Everest with Hillary. I don't know. But I do know I will be doing it with a smile on my face.

Life is about choices, young man. Choose to act or choose to not. Either way you've made a choice. But I hope you choose to live. You're three levels smarter than any boy I've ever met and yet you spend your days with a nose stuck in a video game. This makes your grandfather sad.

So far in your life, most choices have been made for you. I've seen it. You're bored. You're not inspired and you're miserable. Your life can change today…if you come. Join your old Grandpa Wally. Turn around and look into the darkness. Your future can be amazing if you walk into the unknown. Trust your grandfather and go into the darkness.

And the notes had four words: *Chaser, come find me.*

Chase started playing with the rubber bands. Nerves started to take over his body. It seemed like the thing to do. Plus, as long as he kept that up he didn't really have to decide about his next step. Or what that meant. Come find me…**WHERE?!**

His hand started to tremble a little. His heart pumped a little louder…then it was thumping. Almost out of his chest. He had a decision to make. He wondered. He wavered. Until, four words caught his eye: *Chaser, come find me.*

Chase knew what he had to do. He pulled the pen light out of the box. He shoved the two batteries inside and turned it on. The beam was not impressive. No matter. Grandpa needed him. He shoved the cigar box along with the rubber bands deep into his backpack and stood up.

Facing the darkness, the tiny flashlight was overmatched so Chase stood motionless, looking into the dark corner of the basement. The place where the sun never shines. The place where light refuses to shine. The black abyss.

In his other hand, the note from his grandpa. Stuffed in the back of the codebook. He kept looking down at it. The book, nor the letter produced anymore bravery, courage or guts to take another step forward.

What did provide the jolt to young Chase was the wind. Not directly, but it did nonetheless. The wind had picked up so much that the shutters of the old house began slamming against the house. A storm had rolled in. The shutters were the first to feel the brunt of it.

It was the beginning of a loud Midwestern thunderstorm. One that continued all night, but Chase wasn't around to hear the worst of it. Just the first slaps of wood against wood. It caused him to jump forward. Actually, it caused him to leap several steps forward.

Straight into the blackness. He stopped, trying to let his eyes adjust. They never did. It was black.

"Grandpa?" meekly eked from Chase's mouth.

Not a sound...until he heard another shutter slam against the house. The wind howled a little louder. Chase was now two more steps into the blackness and while he couldn't see the book in his hand, he could feel the raised sun on the leather cover. *What was that rule? The sun will always guide you...*

Chase took another step forward...then another...and another. He passed through a doorway, or what felt like a doorway. His foot had bumped something. He almost tripped but caught himself. He felt for something, anything. With his hands. With his foot. Anything.

He slid his foot forward, very slowly, each movement calculated. A few more steps as he timidly inched himself deeper into the darkness. What he couldn't really tell was that he had passed through an opening.

His eyes spotted a glimmer ahead. Something shiny. Barely, but it was a ray of light. Like light coming through a crack. Bolstered by the sight, he took a few more steps.

He was also bolstered by the wind behind him. Because at that moment when his comfort was gaining, the door he just passed through slammed shut.

"AGGHHHH!!!!"

After he peeled himself off the ceiling, he lunged back blindly for the knob. His heart nearly burst from his chest again. Trying to get the knob to turn or unlock just wasn't going to happen. Chase was locked in.

He couldn't go back now. Over his shoulder, the light shone a little brighter through the crack. And light right now was a precious commodity. He turned toward it. The closer he got, the easier it was to make out the source. *Maybe, it was coming from the moon. Maybe, this was the fallout shelter. Maybe that's where I am.* His hopes rose.

Then they fell. Those doors were locked tight. There was no crack in them. *There's no way I'm going to get out of here. Until morning.*

He took a few more steps and leaned in for a closer look. *Wait! The light isn't from the moon but a small little sun that's over the doors. The light is coming from the sun? What?! That's crazy! I'm trapped for sure. And I'm starting to go crazy. If that's not the outside, then I'm deep in the ground. And if I'm deep in the ground, there's no way Mom and Dad are ever going to find me.* More fear washed over Chase. He was scared, then angry, then really, really mad. So mad, he punched the wall. OWW! That hurt!

And he would have been reeling in pain except he heard a crunch. His fist had hit something other than the concrete wall. He focused his penlight straight ahead and flashed it and then his eyes locked on to the object he punched.

IT WAS A PETRIFIED SNAKE! YUK!!!!! Chase wasn't angry anymore. He was freaked out! He backpedaled as fast as he could until his back hit the big metal doors. When he did, his back knocked the lock off easily.

Chase couldn't believe it. *What just happened? Did I just get myself free? That's so cool. I'll be out of here fast and back in bed in minutes.* He pushed open the steel doors...but it wasn't the backyard of the Grandpa's farmhouse. It wasn't moonlight hitting his face. Nope. That was the sun that was blinding him. The sun that shone directly overhead. The sun that burned bright and warm, hot actually. He wasn't in the backyard anymore. He wasn't close.

But where was he?

Chapter 4

"This isn't the Farm..."

Chase knew that for sure. First, because it was hot. Second, it was the middle of the day. And then mainly because when he looked down from the blinding sun, he saw the bluest ocean he'd ever seen. The water was fifty feet below the cliff he was standing upon. He wasn't quite at the edge, but he wasn't that far from it. *Man that ocean is blue. The bluest I've ever seen. Bluer than the ocean at Coney Island. Blue like crayon box blue.*

When he turned around, and it took awhile, he noticed a small one-story building sitting in the middle of a little clearing surrounded by thick bushes and tall trees. A little path ran behind the hut leading into the woods. Not fancy, this little hut had a lot of privacy, unless you consider the wide-open view of the ocean.

Made of stone blocks and plaster, it did not look regal or lavish, rather it looked like the kind of place a guard would be stationed. Someone assigned to watch the sea and warn the surrounding villages if outsiders were approaching. It's where a military man would gaze for hours at the open sea and then alert the nearby army that the enemy was advancing.

When he walked around the hut to explore, he noticed two things he hadn't before: a long spear, sharp and pointed and a long bow leaning against the front wall. This <u>was</u> a military outpost...or maybe the hunting home of a very angry loner. The kind of guy who hates visitors. The kind of guy who wants to be left alone and will stop at nothing to get it.

Chase got a shiver up his spine. He would be considered an outsider. He would definitely not be wanted. In fact, he'd probably feel the business end of that spear. No need to get poked. No need at all.

He quickly moved to the side of the structure. Out of view of the path and most of the ocean cliff. He listened very quietly. Besides the thump-thump of his heart, he swore he heard nothing. Maybe he was lucky. Maybe no one was around. At least he couldn't be seen or heard by anyone. Then again, who would hear him here? And where was here?

Maybe the guy was out hunting or inside taking a nap. Chase had to investigate. He worked up the courage to poke his nose into the open window. A window that was just an opening, no glass, no wood, just a hole. Not really that secure, but maybe in this place, it was ok to leave your house unguarded. Maybe if you were a guard, it didn't matter. Inside, the hut was mainly empty...and a mess. A few mats thrown around and a linen sheet hanging from the back window. A few dirty, clay pots and cups and a nasty looking pair of sandals. This guy was a slob…and if his clothes meant anything, Chase bet he looked like one of those hippie/homeless guys that lived on the street corner back in New York.

There was a small fire just outside the back of the hut. Chase could hear the small crackle and pop of a fire. As he approached, something in a small clay pot was bubbling. It wasn't pleasant smelling, then again it wasn't all that bad smelling either. But he was definitely glad he didn't have to eat or drink it.

A moment of investigation and his internal radar went off. Something told him that trouble was nearby. The more he thought, the more he wasn't feeling safe…or happy. He definitely wasn't glad he found the fire. That meant someone was nearby. And that meant he needed to hide quickly. He didn't know where he was, but he didn't need anyone else to know where he was either. As confused as he was, he was more scared.

That fear exploded when the bushes nearest to him began to shake. Something was coming! A person, an animal…an army. Chase ran behind the hut, his heart beating a million miles an hour. He peeked around the corner. The bush had stopped moving. Maybe it was an animal. He glanced behind him. Still sitting along the hut wall was the spear. Chase did not hesitate. His left hand wrapped around the shaft of the spear. He was no longer unarmed.

He felt a little better…until the same bush began to shake again. Then the one next to it. Now two bushes were shaking…as were Chase's hands.

His head peeked around the corner once more. His eyes glued on the bushes, his heart beating through his chest. Then the bushes stopped. Chase couldn't move his eyes. Everything was calm. He took a deep breath. Then he leaned back. His head and back resting against the hut. Another deep breath. His eyes closed for a moment. *What was he going to do? What if this guy comes back? What is going on? Where am I?* Another deep breath.

In Greek, "HELLO?"

Chase's eyes popped open. His hands flinched. His legs clenched. He thrust the spear out and dropped into a crouch. Standing on the other side of the spear was a young man wearing a tunic and sandals. To Chase, he looked 13 or 14. He was slightly bigger than Chase, but not a huge boy. This boy's hands were raised in a defensive position in reaction to the spear but he was not attacking Chase.

"Eirene. Philos." He slowly stepped back.

Chase hadn't moved...or taken a breath. He was still crouched in a fearful attack like position, aiming the spear directly at the visitor.

"Eirene."

"Is that English?"

The boy repeated his word, "Eirene."

Chase thought he had heard that word. It wasn't English but he knew he knew that word. "Eirene?"

The boy nodded yes.

Chase repeated it again, "eirene?" Again the boy nodded.

"Peace?" The other boy was now confused at the English translation but he tried to repeat Chase's word.

"Peace?"

Now Chase nodded. "Eirene...Peace."

The older boy was more confident in his speech. "Peace."

When Chase heard the word peace this time, he unclenched slightly. When he looked at this boy's eyes, he began to believe he meant it. There was a gentle quality to his face and his stance. He was not threatening. Especially when he retreated a few more steps back.

"Mastic?"

"What?" Chase responded.

"Mastic." The older boy pointed toward the fire.

Chase glanced over at the fire and the pot hanging over it but he kept one lingering eye on this stranger.

The older boy began speaking in Greek. Ancient Greek. And Chase tried to listen. He was surprised that he actually understood a few words. The nouns mostly but he was getting them.

Fotia = fire. Spiti = house/home. Man = Anthropos. Then the boy said "Mastic" again.

"Mastic?" That didn't register to Chase.

In Greek the boy continued, "I'm drying it over by the fire. I apologize, I entered your camp. I was walking by and noticed the mastic shrubs. I just wanted something to soothe my stomach."

A big smile came across the older boy's face. "Mastic is very good for your mouth." The boy walked right past Chase and his still outstretched spear. He headed straight for the fire.

Reaching into a small pot, he produced a small white substance. It looked a little rubbery as he put it in his mouth. He then offered some to Chase. Chase squinted. Leery. Very leery. But the boy kept chewing.

The Greek boy offered it to his new friend. "Taste it."

Chase had seen a few late-night detective movies in his life. He knew he had to be cautious.

"You want me to eat that?" Chase was skeptical. The boy nodded. Chase took a small portion and popped it in his mouth. He chewed...and swallowed. The boy was quick to shake his head no. He made the motion to chew but not to swallow. "No. You don't swallow it. You just chew it. See, the mastic continues to give you a spice taste for quite some time."

"Are you kidding me?"

The boy was not.

"Are you making chewing gum?"

"Gum?"

"Gum. You chew it for flavor but never swallow..."

"If that's what you call gum, then yes, that is what I'm making." They were having a conversation but both spoke in different languages. A lot of it was acted out. It was Greek and English charades. But the Greek boy was smart and he was picking up Chase's language. And at the same time, Chase's Latin and Greek lessons were kicking in.

Chase took the offering again and put it in his mouth. Not quite Bubble Yum Citrus Explosion, but not as bad as it smelt earlier. Kind of like that lame chewing gum he always found in the back of his Grandpa's kitchen drawer.

Then Ari asked, "This isn't your camp?"

The boy shook his head.

"Is it yours?"

Chase shook his head as well.

"So my new friend, you are not from here?"

Chase shook his head no.

"I guess I should have known that."

"Why?" Chase asked.

"You dress very strange."

Chase was thinking the same thing. The two eyed each other up and down.

"Where are you from?

"New York."

"New York...I have not heard of such a place. Is it near Syracuse?"

"Sort of...five, six hours away by car — "

" — by what?"

"By cart."

"Cart?"

"Ah...yes. By cart."

The boy in the tunic nodded in understanding. "I see...and yet you dress very strangely for a Greek."

"Greek? I'm in Greece?!"

"Yes you are. As you would be if you were in Syracuse." The boy in the tunic looked him over more suspiciously. "Where is this New York really located?"

"Ah...overseas. Far away from here." Then Chase realized he needed to change the subject. "My name is Chase. What's yours?"

"I am called Ari. Or I like to be. My full name is Aristotle of Athens, son of Nicomachus, personal physician to King Amyntas of Macedon."

"I'm Chase Axelrod from the Upper West Side. Son of Trent and Theresa Axelrod, importer and exporters, Java Bytes Unlimited."

Ari paused for a moment in thought, "So you must have run away from home."

Chase didn't realize it as he answered but he began to unload his whole story. "Well, I didn't try. It just sort of happened. I just walked through the fallout shelter doors and then it just sort of put me here. I'm just looking for my Grandfather. Have you seen him?"

"I'm afraid I haven't seen anyone today except you."

Chase nodded and paced around. *What was he going to do?* He sat down on the edge of the cliff, overlooking the sea. Ari joined him.

"So this is Athens? I expected it to be bigger."

"This is not Athens. We are a day's walk from Athens."

Chase was silent.

"Is Athens your destination?"

"I don't know."

The boys were silent again until Chase asked, "Are you on a trip?"

Ari answered sheepishly, "Actually I tend to walk when I think. Sometimes I look up and I've walked a fairly long distance. That is what happened today. I came upon this outpost and saw the mastic bushes. I knew I couldn't wait all day for the resin to dry so I made a fire to speed up the process."

"Sounds like some good science."

"Science?"

"Science. Yeah…you know. Experiments. Biology. Chemistry. Physics. Science."

"I have heard of these disciplines. I've just never heard of them called science."

"Oh." Chase clammed up. One of the rules from the little blue leather book popped into his head. *Did he just say something wrong? Did he just overstep his bounds?*

"Please keep speaking. I am interested in your wisdom. I can't wait to tell my fellow students of this strange visitor I met in Megara."

"Oh no! Please don't speak of me at all! I'm not supposed to be here. I mean…I am but I'm not. I'm not supposed to change anything. Or disturb anything."

"That wasn't you in the hut? Because that looks disturbed."

"I didn't touch a thing."

Both of the boys' brains were racing but neither said anything.

"Well, my stomach has more needs than the mastic. Are you hungry?"

Chase pondered before shaking his head yes.

Ari and Chase entered the hut and searched for anything edible but their quest ended with only a few, slightly dried-out olives.

"Not the meal I was hoping for. You would think an outpost would have more supplies. That must be why the resident has left."

"Do you think he will be back soon?"

"Within a day or two. Depending on where he has decided to go."

At that moment, the two boys heard a soft rumble. They exited the hut to get a better look, pausing outside to listen. The rumble was still low and very hard to make out. The waves lapping the beach did not help. Ari, taking the lead, moved down the path to another clearing. They still couldn't make out the sound so they moved through the heavy brush. Down the long and winding path, the makers of the sound began to appear. It was an army! A heavily-armed military marching. Ari dropped to the ground and seconds later pulled Chase down too.

"Are you a soldier?"

Chase said no.

"Is that why you are dressed so strangely?"

Chase protested, "I'm not a soldier."

"Because those are your people."

"My people?!"

"The Spartan army. You said you were from Syracuse. The upper west side."

"I did, but not that—"

"—well you are very old not to be from Sparta and a soldier. If they spot you, you will be made a soldier and asked to fight."

"Fight?! Me?! Fight who?"

"They usually make boys into soldiers at age seven. You are far older than that." Ari and Chase continued to study the marching troops as they grew closer. Ari continued, "They are obviously marching to battle."

"To battle? Where?" Athens?"

"No, Athens and Sparta are not at war. Not again, anyway. My guess is Thebes. There has been rumor of war between those two cities."

"Thebes, where is that?"

"It is to the north. Another day's walk."

"Why are they fighting?"

"Because the Spartans know nothing but war. It is their industry."

"That's all they do?"

"My father used to say, be sad for the people that know nothing but war. They are a people of small spirit and short sight."

The boys watched for a few more moments before Ari urged them to leave. "If they hear us, we may both be drafted. Being a citizen of Athens, I have no friend or enemy in this battle. And I choose not to fight a war for which I am not invested."

Chase nodded in agreement.

Ari crawled off, staying low. Chase followed. Closely.

The two reached the first clearing before getting to their feet. Hustling off toward the hut, Chase grabbed Ari's arm. "Are you sure we should go back to the hut?"

"We must put out the fire before they see or smell it. If we don't, they will know people are around."

The boys reached the fire quickly, stamping it out and covering it with dirt. Once that was complete, they needed an alternative escape route. The main path would lead to the main road and by now it would be full of Spartan soldiers.

"Which way?" Chase asked.

"I am thinking."

"Don't think too much!"

The boys looked up to see two Spartan soldiers walking out of the hut.

Chapter 5

"I'm not a Spy!"

The boys tried to plead that to their captors but it was not accepted. Nope. Ari and Chase were tied together, back to back, to one of the logs that supported the main structure of the hut with one of the linen window shades. The Spartan soldiers were irritated with their young prisoners, irritated mainly that they tried to run, causing them to chase after and finally catch them. Not only had the boys evaded capture for so long that the marching army had passed, but the guys had ran so far down the opposite path and into such treacherous terrain that one of the soldiers had twisted his ankle while the other one fell and scrapped his entire arm on the rocks. They were mad. And hungry. And as night fell, they were left behind to catch up to the main army tomorrow.

The soldiers solved the hunger issue first. They raided the nearby farm and stole a goat. They had built the fire back up and were now roasting that goat on a spit. As the soldiers talked near the fire, Ari and Chase worried they may be outfitted for war when day broke.

"Where are they going to take us?"

"I heard the one say Leuctra."

"Where's that?"

"North of here."

"Near your home?"

"No. Athens is east. Leuctra is in Thebes. And right now the Spartans are attacking them at Leuctra. Athens fought the Spartans 16 years ago in the Corinthian War. Lasted twelve years. It was Sparta against a coalition of states: Thebes, Athens, Corinth, and Argos. Before that it was the Peloponnesian War where Athens fought against the Peloponnesian League, led by Sparta. Right now, Athens is at peace but I'm sure we will fight them again...and soon."

"What are you fighting for?"

"Have you heard of democracy?"

"Yeah, of course."

"You have?"

"Yeah."

"I thought it only existed here in Athens."

"My country is a democra—" Chase stopped. "I've heard of it. So that's why you're fighting?"

"Simply put, democracy versus oligarchy."

"The war is that simple?"

"Well, we have democracy and the Spartans have an oligarchy."

"Oligarchy?"

"Where the same small group of people always rule. Forever."

Chase said nothing.

"I guess our cities just look at the world differently. Our cultures are very different."

"How so?"

"The Spartans are warriors. They look at the world with the warrior's eyes. They are trained from a very young age to fight. At seven or eight they join the army."

"In the army? At seven or eight?" Chase was amazed.

"They live in barracks. Away from home. They are treated very harshly. Young kids are beaten by older children. They think this makes them strong. They're whipped and beaten and given very little food. It makes them wild like dogs. Stealing food. They learn to cheat and steal to survive. But it makes them better fighters."

Chase looked over to see the soldiers eating like dogs. Their teeth ripping the meat of the bones. They looked mean and vicious. "I guess so…" Worry crept into Chase. Ari saw this.

"They endure a lot of pain. But their leaders want it that way. They are ruled by fear."

"And your country is different."

"My city."

"The Spartans _are_ Greeks. Well, they speak Greek, write Greek, but they are much different. In Athens, we make our children students not soldiers. We value art and music and poetry. We only fight when we must."

"I'd like to see Athens."

"I'll show you tomorrow."

Chase looks at Ari like he's crazy. "How? We'll be fighting for the Spartans tomorrow."

"We must use our brains to escape this."

"Ok, and like I just asked, how?"

"That I don't know, but soon those two will fall asleep on a full stomach and their sleep will be deep. That is our moment to act."

Hours later Chase was staring at the stars over the Sardonic Gulf. The waves crashed below the cliff as the thoughts of helplessness rolled through his brain. He certainly didn't want to fight. He could get killed. Not video game killed, but really killed! Then Chase hoped that Ari was smart enough to get them out of this mess. At that moment, Chase felt a nudge. Ari whispered that he thought the soldiers were asleep.

"What are we going to do?" Chase asked.

"I don't know."

"You don't?"

"I'm not a criminal. I've never been tied up. I am from the upper class. What do _you_ think we should do?"

"You think _I'm_ a criminal?"

"You look like you could be." Chase was confused at Ari's words. "I think you look like a soldier. I think you come from another country. And I don't think you look like a Greek citizen. So you're far from home with no money and you say you have no idea where you are. Either you are from the stars or a liar. If you're a liar, then you're probably a thief as well. I suggest you use your thievery to get us loose."

Chase. Was. Steaming. He was not a thief. He was not a criminal. And he was not a liar! But at this moment, Ari's opinion did not matter. Right now, he must get free so tomorrow morning he was actually not a soldier, fighting in a war he knew nothing about, nor cared who won. He just wanted to find his grandfather and find his way out of this place.

Ari added insult to injury, "I bet your container is full of stolen items."

BOOM! Chase's eyes opened. "Can you reach my backpack?"

"Backpack?"

"Backpack. Bag. Satchel. Pouch. Container. Whatever you call it."

"Well, maybe. Hold on." Ari stretched with his foot. The bag leaned against the hut where Chase had dropped it when Ari originally scared the feathers off him.

Now, Ari's legs were just inches short of reaching the backpack. Chase, craning over his shoulder, saw the unsuccessful attempts.

"Try it without the sandals." Ari did and increased his reach slightly but not quite far enough. His big toe could graze the pack but couldn't hook the closest arm strap.

Ari's voice lowered, "I am not long enough."

"Not yet."

Now Ari was confused.

"We can lengthen you by scrunching down, way down. I learned this in gym."

"Scrunching?"

"Yes. Scrunching?"

"What does that mean?"

"Uh...scrunching...just slide closer to the ground. To the Earth."

Chase and Ari both scooted down on their backs, lifting their arms as far as they could above their head. This stretch of their arms put a tremendous amount of stress on their necks, shoulders and arms. And it hurt. It hurt bad. The pain made Chase moan. The longer it took, the more it hurt and the more Chase wanted to scream out in agony.

"Hurry up!" He screamed in a whisper.

The first swing of his leg came up short. Then Ari strained a little farther and reached a little farther. And again, he was unsuccessful. Chase tried to swallow the pain.

"Just a little more." Ari requested.

"HURRY!" Chase coughed up. The guards shifted slightly. The boys froze. They watched the soldiers slowly fall back asleep. The boys paused to let the guards fall deeper then resumed their quest for freedom.

Chase gulped a deep breath and got down as low as he could. Then he dug in a little deeper. Ari knew this would be his best chance. He also dug as deep into the ground with his back as he could. He stretched farther than he ever stretched and his toe snagged the closest strap. He pulled it a few inches closer...then a few more and finally the backpack sat in his lap.

"Got it!" Ari excitedly yelped. And yelped a little too loud because one of the soldiers heard his voice. Ari saw this. Chase saw this. And when the guard sat up, he saw them. He began to rise and investigate the ruckus.

"Give it to me!"

Ari nudged the backpack to Chase's hands and he quickly tried to dig inside the bag. His hands furiously dug through the bag. He was trying to find the cigar box and inside it, the buck knife.

His hand searched blindly for the knife, but the guard got to them first. His scowl was mean, mean and ominous. His eyes burned into theirs. Maybe these boys wouldn't be fighting tomorrow. Maybe this guard would smash their heads at this moment.

His eyes spotted the movement of Chase's hands. He knelt down to get a better look. Chase's hands moved slightly…but enough. The guard began to reach for the pack when he suddenly….PFFFFTTTTT!

The guard fell back in pain. He was howling.

Chase quickly grabbed the cigar box, wedged his hand inside and grabbed the knife. He flipped it open in one motion. He sliced the linen, freeing both Ari and himself.

"What happened?" Ari asked.

"He found himself on the wrong end of a rubber band! C'mon!"

Chase grabbed the backpack and they tore off into the woods. The soldier recovered even though his eye stung from a direct hit to the pupil. His partner heard the screams, woke up and tore off running.

Chase and Ari had a head start but the soldiers were well trained fighting machines. They grabbed their spears and swords, running quickly after the escapees.

The forest was thick and dense...dark. The branches hung low and more than a few times hit Chase right across the face. And when he wasn't taking a beating from the trees and shrubs, his feet hit divots and bumps on the uneven ground. He focused forward to Ari running faster and faster away from him and glanced behind him to see the soldiers running faster and faster toward him. Something had to change or he was going to be tied up to the hut again very soon.

Only feet away, the one-eyed guard lunged at Chase. Luckily, he was glancing over his shoulder and jumped to his right. The guard missed. And he hit the ground, swallowing a mouthful of dirt and shrub. Chase was lucky. And now he had another few steps between him and the pursuing soldier. Then again, maybe he wasn't so lucky. When he turned to dive out of the way, he turned toward the ocean...or rather, the cliff.

If the moon hadn't been so bright that night, Chase may not have seen the edge...or the big stone that caused him to trip and in turn stop his forward momentum. He went down. Skinned his knee. Biffed on his left side. And generally looked like a fool. But the one thing he did not do was run over the edge. And he did not fall hundreds of feet below into the water or on the beach. He caught himself. The one-eyed soldier chasing him had only one good eye. And that's because the other one was still stinging from the rubber band. And because it was still stinging, he could not judge depth. He might have judged depth better in the midday sun, but at night...

Chase heard him fly by. Chase heard him slowly fall into the black. And Chase heard a small, distant splash. Chase knew he and his nemesis would no longer have any problems. Chase Axelrod had outwitted and outperformed a Spartan soldier. *Wait 'til Grandpa Wally heard about that!*

As he pulled himself up to higher ground, he set forth to find Ari and potentially fight another guard. Five minutes of wandering through a dark forest had got him nowhere but lost. He had no idea where Ari was or where he was.

Thirty minutes later, he still had no idea of anything. But he kept walking…slowly and cautiously. You never knew what might be lurking around the next hill. He took some time going left and then right and then left again. By the time he had spent nearly two hours alone in the forest, he didn't care who found him anymore.

It was about this time that Chase saw a glimmer of light ahead. LIGHT! That meant somebody was there that could help him. He hoped. He snuck quietly as he could through the brush, pushing away shrubs and ducking under tree branches. As he neared the light, he saw a very familiar sight. It was the hut. The same hut he originally walked out of. Then he saw an even better sight. Ari. Sitting next to the fire. Eating a piece of roasted goat. And near the hut: the other soldier. Tied up and unconscious. Chase smiled for the first time since he arrived in ancient Greece.

"Chase!" Ari cried out as Chase appeared from the forest.

"Ari, how did you…?"

"Physics!"

"Physics?"

"Well, the power of a large tree branch pulled to the point of almost breaking. And when the soldier finds the perfect spot: SPPPLAATTTT!"

Chase giggled at Ari getting so animated. He would later learn he was in the presence of one of the greatest mind's in the history of the world and he just heard him say, "SPPPLAATTTT!"

Chase sat with his new friend and enjoyed some of the roasted goat along with a few olives and water that Ari had found in the soldier's supplies. They rested and ate and enjoyed the time together.

As day broke in the East, Chase told Ari he needed to return to his Grandfather's house. Ari told him that he would help him.

"I don't know if I need any help. I think I just need to go back through the doorway with the sun symbol and I'll be fine." This exclamation caught Ari by surprise and Chase knew he needed to explain. At least, a little. He swore the young Greek to the solemn promise of silence. Once he had his new friend's word, he began to explain the last twelve hours of his life. At least, he thought it was twelve hours. He really had no idea how long he had been in ancient Greece or just how long he was gone from rural Minnesota. *I mean, what was a few hours when he had traveled back two thousand, three hundred and eighty-one years?*

Chase stopped again and made Ari again affirm his solemn promise of silence. At first, Ari took a small offense. When Chase explained it was not personal, Ari relented and promised once more.

He told him about the basement and about the fallout shelter and he told him about the sun symbol and he told him about Grandpa Wally. He showed him the codebook and they both sat quietly and thought when they weren't shouting out ideas.

Chase thought he needed to go through the same door. And they tried to walk in and out of the front door of the hut. They walked in and out of the back door of the hut as well but neither worked. They were stumped. And now the sun was rising higher and higher in the sky. Ari told him that another army might march by at any time. Plus, he was expected back home soon. Then a light went off in Ari's mind. And he shouted the best answer he could ever imagine.

"Athens!"

"Athens?"

"If your Grandfather is as intelligent and astute as you say he is, there is no way he would have lead you to Greece without making you see the jewel of Greece."

Chase thought about it. He had heard quite a bit about Athens. And not just from Grandpa and the video game he had given Chase. They talked about it in Latin and Greek class. In history class. Even in that Civilization game his Dad played a few years ago on the computer.

"You told me last night you'd like to see it."

"OK, Athens. That's sounds logical."

Ari cocked his head when Chase said the word, logical.

Chase paid him no attention. "Let's go."

Ari snapped to, "Great! But first we need to change your clothes."

"Why?"

"Because wearing that, you'll stand out."

Chapter 6

"I'm <u>NOT</u> wearing a dress!"

"It's not a dress, it's a tunic!"

"Well, I'm not wearing a tunic either."

"But you'll stand out!"

"So."

"So, they will either consider you a Spartan and jail you or call you heretic and stone you to death. Which would you prefer?"

"I thought you said Athens was a city of intelligence!"

"It is. But crazy is still crazy. And the scared masses are still led by the weakest and most fearful minds."

Chase had no reply to that. So he went into the hut to change but he did not go happily. And when he came out, he was wearing a homemade tunic. And he sorta looked like a Greek man. Like most tunics, it was linen. And it came down to his knees. His lower legs were bare. As were his feet. And while a lot of Greek men were barefoot, the walk was long and over dusty and rocky paths. Ari had found him some sandals, the pair that used to be worn by the tied-up soldier.

Their walk to Athens started early but it would still take them most of the day. And in this time, they passed over the rocky and rugged terrain that was Greece. They passed groves of olive trees and fields that were more dirt than plants. Ari explained the rocky conditions made it very hard on farmers. He told them most people that lived near the gulf, survived on the harvest of the sea. "One must walk inland to find fields that fed."

Chase enjoyed the guided tour he was receiving but too many facts and not enough stories. This caused his eyes to gloss over. Plus, he was also getting irritated by the blisters that were forming on his feet. Those sandals were far from comfortable. He never mentioned it to Ari but ancient Greece was not better than 21st century America when it came to footwear. Chase's idea of "Nike" was much different than Ari's. In ancient Greece, Nike wasn't a pair of sneakers. It was the Greek God of Victory.

Ari noticed his friend's distance and changed the subject. "So you're looking for your grandfather?"

Chase quickly responded, "Yes."

"Why do you think he sent you to Greece?"

"I don't know. It has one of the most famous cities in the world. And one of the oldest. And I know it was important in creating art and thought and architecture...but I can't say exactly. I guess there is a lot to see so he's probably in some museum waiting for me. Waiting to tell me a story about a sculpture or a building or some great person."

"If he's there looking for a great person, there's none greater than my master, Plato."

"Plato's your master? Are you a slave or something?"

"No. I'm his pupil...or I will be. In a few years, when I turn eighteen years. Then I will be ready for his Academy."

"You look very excited."

"That I am, Chase. That I am."

"Plato is the finest mind. His intelligence is unmatched."

Chase listened as Ari continued. "You know, he studied at the feet of Socrates. The first great philosopher of Greece!"

"I have heard of him."

"Of course you have. Everyone should be familiar with his thoughts. Master Plato is a genius."

The journey from the hut to Athens had neared its end. The two boys crested one of the outlying hills to see the entire city-state of Athens. On the skyline, two things towered above, Mount Lycabettus and the Acropolis highlighted by the Parthenon.

"If anyone asks, you are my slave and you don't speak."

"What?"

Ari provided no more explanation. He had already begun down the rocky road into the city. He ran, and quick, so excited to return to his home. What Chase wouldn't give to come over a hill and see Central Park or the Empire State Building or even his Grandpa's farmhouse. He'd love to see that old house on the hilltop like he did yesterday...or twenty hours ago...or whenever he was back in the fields of Minnesota. *What he wouldn't give!*

The young men wove their way through the busy and crowded streets of Athens. It was late afternoon. And the merchants were selling everything they could before the sun set on their day. Meats, olives, clothing, wine, anything a person in Athens would need to survive. The hustle and bustle of these streets reminded Chase of the streets and markets of his hometown of New York. The chaos soothed him slightly. It was the first time on this journey that he'd had that feeling.

Ari asked, "Where do you think we should start?"

"The book says the highest or tallest building in the land."

"Why didn't you say so?! I know exactly where your portal lies."

"Where?"

"The Parthenon!"

Again, Ari was almost running through the streets. And Chase tried to keep pace but his blisters were growing with each step and so was the pain. They passed the Academy and Ari slammed on the brakes. He stood, staring at the small doorway leading to a garden-like grove. He peered around the corner as Chase waited on him to start running again.

"My master teaches in there. Here, look."

Both boys stuck their noses around the corner to see a group of young men sitting around an older man. He was in the middle of a discussion.

They tried to stand quietly in back, hoping not to be seen, but Ari couldn't contain his excitement. He continued his verbal tour of the Academy. "We are trained in the arts and the sciences. We learn poetry, drama, reading and writing. We study the sciences. And mathematics. We play music and art. It is the greatest site of learning a boy can ever attend."

Ari's passion got the best of him and he leaned in for another chance to hear the words of Plato. He craned his head inside but couldn't make out the words. That didn't stop him. He took a few steps inside. Chase, not wanting to lose Ari, followed close behind. Soon, they were standing just feet outside the circle. Plato seemed not to mind so Ari motioned Chase to sit.

As much as Chase would like to get to their destination, his feet were overjoyed for the rest. He removed the sandals and began rubbing his feet. As the pain eased, he started to hear more and more of what this older man was saying. He wasn't paying complete attention. It was difficult. Chase didn't understand some of Plato's words. The lesson was a little over his head so he started to drift off, thinking about his quest to find his Grandpa. To him, it sounded like another boring lecture from Mrs. Thatcher.

"My teacher, Socrates, once said, 'wisdom begins in wonder.' I truly believe this search for wisdom is the true purpose of his life. Because, as Socrates said, it's not living that matters, but living rightly."

Chase's attention had moved to his backpack. Inside, shoved underneath his clothes and tennis shoes, sat the cigar box. Under that, the object of his search: his DS. He slowly removed it and pressed the 'ON' button. The device booted up. As it did, a few beeps eked out before he could mute the device. He snuck a quick look around and noticed that the class had lost its focus of the teacher. Chase started his game and solved "this world" in no time flat. Waiting for the second world to load, he rubbed his feet again. They were still sore. At this moment, he heard another lesson from Plato, "If a man neglects his education, he walks lame to the end of his life."

Chase got nudged in the arm. He looked up to see Plato staring at him. Laser-like. Chase slowly slid the DS into the backpack. Plato continued, "And with wisdom, comes courage. Courage that allows us to act. It is courage that helps us overcome that of which we are scared. See men, courage is knowing what not to fear. And when we know what not to fear, well, courage is then a salvation."

Chase was locked in on the teacher at this moment. Plato looked around at the boys. "I think these words are enough for today. I ask you to ponder them and sit and think. Search your minds and your souls and we will discuss tomorrow morning. The sun sets in an hour or so. We will end the lessons today."

Chase grabbed Ari's arm, "We have to get going."

"But I'd like to speak with the master."

"How about tomorrow? There's only a few hours of sunlight."

"You don't know if it has to be found in daytime."

"I don't know that it doesn't. The book says, *The Sun will Always Guide You!*"

Ari could see that Chase was moving from antsy to angry.

"Fine." Much to the chagrin of Ari, they quickly ran down the streets of Athens toward the temple on the hill.

As the boys reached the base of the hill, Chase had a question for his Greek friend, "Why were there no girls in that class?"

Ari laughed, "Girls don't go to school! Are you crazy?!"

"I go to school with girls."

Ari was shocked. "Why?"

"Because...I don't know. Because...I do."

They began the rocky climb up the steep path.

Ari questioned Chase, "And you don't think that's a bit odd?"

"No. It's the way it's always been."

"Well, in this city, boys go to school. Girls stay at home with their mothers."

"Why?"

"They're not educated."

Now, Chase was blown away, "You're saying women aren't smart."

"That's exactly what I'm saying. They're crazy, irrational. They get hysterical."

"Well, I'm not a big fan of girls either but they aren't as crazy as you think. They're some of the smartest people in my class."

"Men think clearly. Women do not."

Chase couldn't believe he was defending a girl, let alone the whole gender, "I think if you ever came to my school, you'd think a lot differently."

"I find that hard to believe."

Chase had had enough. "Let's get going. The sun is setting."

Ari and Chase climbed to the top of the Acropolis to find themselves standing in front of the Parthenon.

"They built this as a temple to Athena."

"Isn't she just a myth?"

Ari looked at Chase with a glare. "She's the goddess of wisdom. I guess your people do not value wisdom!"

"We value wisdom. We just don't worship a goddess for it."

Just then, they reached the steps of the Parthenon. Behind them, the most amazing view of Athens, its neighborhoods, houses, buildings and in the distance, the sea. It was an amazing view, even for Chase. He reached into his backpack, producing his DS and snapped a picture. He would have taken more if the sun was not hanging so low in the sky. As he and Ari turned around, they were dwarfed by the massive stone columns directly in front of them.

They stared. Upward. Really far upward. The columns look like they touch the sky. If not for the roof, they probably would.

"Let us go inside."

They guys walked in, past a few mingling people and the awe with the Parthenon continued.

The columns. The sculptures. The colors. The height and size of everything. He had seen the skyscrapers in Manhattan and he had been to Yankee Stadium and The Garden but this place was impressive. More impressive than all those. "This place is huge. How are we going to find the portal?"

Ari had no clue but he also didn't seem as concerned about it. "Have you ever thought that maybe your Grandpa wanted you to stay here and wait for him?"

Chase hadn't. And now he had something else to think about. Maybe his Grandpa was coming. To meet him. And he was just supposed to hang out. Go to Plato's Academy some more. Learn from one of the smartest minds in history. And study with one of the other great minds. I mean, his new friend was Aristotle. *Why was he in such a hurry to get out of here?*

From Chase's silence, Ari could tell he just flipped Chase's world. "My apologies."

Chase looked over at his buddy. "No worries."

Changing the subject, Ari suggested they should just look for the portal. It doesn't mean he had to go through it. "Just knowing where it is, is a good thing."

Chase agreed. "But every opening between the columns could be the portal."

"I doubt that. If this is really a portal to another place or time, it will be special. It will stand alone and you will know."

"You're probably right. That seems logical."

"You used that word before. What does it mean?

"Logical? It comes from the word, logic. Reasoned thought. Using many facts that make sense to come to a conclusion. Kinda like the scientific method."

"The scientific method?"

"Yeah. You know, where you gather a bunch of data. Through experiments and observation. You know, evidence that something is true. Then you make a hypothesis, like every day the sun rises in the East so tomorrow the sun will again rise in the East."

That made Aristole stop...and really think, "I like that. May I quote you?"

"You're not quoting me. That's as old as, well...I guess it goes back to ancient Gree--." Chase stopped talking. "I've said way too much."

"NOT AT ALL! Keep going."

Chase remembered another rule, the first rule, about not affecting the world's natural course.

"We gotta find that portal."

Ari was still processing and that was cool with Chase. Whatever happened after he left this world was beyond his control.

Chase spotted a doorway leading into a smaller room. "What's inside here?"

Ari snapped to, "Oh yes! We should check out this room, from what I remember it is..."

"Cool?" Chase finished his sentence. Ari nodded, thinking that "cool" meant something good.

Cool was an understatement. The sculptures in the middle of the enormous main room and the ornate carvings in the wall were cool but when they entered the smaller, inside room, the colors exploded from the wall. This room was cozier than the open air surrounding shell and had a lower ceiling. But it looked no less impressive. That was because it had a long strip of paintings and carvings that told a story of some sort. Chase didn't know that much Greek history so he couldn't make out any particular facts but it was definitely about a battle...or several battles. There were soldiers and horses. They were chariots and swords. They were knights and young men. And they all looked to be moving from the southwest corner of the Parthenon to the north and east. The journey continued.

"This is really long."

And it was. Probably 500 feet long. And three feet high and ran along the upper half of the wall.

"What's it showing?"

Ari didn't know. "I guess that's up for interpretation. The victories of Athens. The wars that saved the cities in the time of Pericles. With the help from Athena."

"Who's Pericles?"

"The first citizen of Athens!" Ari continued, "A famous military general. He saved Athens in the Peloponnesian War and started the construction of this building."

"He sounds cool."

"He was loved by all."

The guys walked farther down the strip. Ari's monologue continued. "This looks more like Athena. And other gods and goddesses."

Chase had moved farther ahead of his friend. He was not as concerned with every little piece of trivia.

"ARI!"

Ari approached the end of the paintings. The last section had already captured Chase's attention. They were at the end of the painting because they were at the end of the room. And the end of the room was a door. But before one came to that door, in the last section of the painting, something else had caught Chase's eye.

"What?"

"The burning boat."

"I don't get it."

"The burning boat. Burning your boats. Nowhere to go but forward. No turning back. Cortes."

"Who?"

Chase sighed, "never mind. Never mind. It's a sign."

"It's a painting."

"No, it's a sign from my Grandpa."

"And what is he saying?"

"He's saying I have to go forward."

"You think this is the portal?"

"Yeah. Look!" Above the huge opening was the small carving. Not an original carving but the sun symbol nonetheless.

"That's a sun."

Ari nodded in agreement.

"So if I walk through this…"

Chase was about to take a few steps forward into the opening when Ari grabbed his arm. "Wait!" Ari extended his hand. They shook. Then he turned, about to walk through again. But he stopped. "What if this works? I may never see you again."

Ari had an answer. "If we do not, then I am better for meeting you. Chase, friendship is a single soul dwelling in two bodies. We will always be friends, no matter where you go."

Chase nodded. And took a step. And another. And another. And then he was no longer standing in the Parthenon. Or Athens. And when he looked behind him, the young Aristotle had disappeared. Actually, when he looked back, he saw nothing. Black. Pitch black. And when he turned back forward, he saw a flash. A huge flash…like an explosion. "Holy Heavens! Who is that? I thought we locked that door!"

"We did, Sir."

"Doesn't look like it to me!"

The flash of blinding light finally left Chase's eyes. And when it did, he noticed that several men in lab coats stood, staring at him. And behind them, an old white haired man standing beside a very old looking light bulb.

"Is this a joke?!" said the old man.

The others, definitely subordinates, began to rush toward Chase.

"Get Julius Caesar out of here!"

Chapter 7

"Julius Caesar?"

"Why are you...?!"

Chase looked down. He was still dressed in the tunic from ancient Greece. But this was the least of his problems. Several large and angry men in white coats began to approach! Chase had only one reaction: Run!

Freaked, he ducked to his left, then sidestepped to his right. He was confused. And scared. And disoriented. But that didn't stop him from running. And quickly evading...the men in white. He didn't, however, avoid the other things that got in his way.

The laboratory warehouse was beyond cluttered. As Chase tried to find his escape, he knocked several things over. Experiments, a bookshelf, and several stands holding what looked like ancient light bulbs and lamps. Instead of capturing the boy, the lab assistants dove to save the years of hard work built by trial and error.

Chase juked and bobbed his way through the gauntlet, passing the current object of their attention, a very ancient looking film projector and found the back door that he had just entered.

But Chase didn't just find it, he crashed through it. The door that is. As he did, another beam of light hit him in the face. But this one wasn't a film projector. This was the sun. He was outside and it was a sunny afternoon. He ducked around the side of the building from which he just escaped and finally had a moment to take a breath and relax.

"Who are you?"

Chase tensed up. The voice sounded forceful. And in charge. And angry. He turned but didn't find another one of the white coats. What he found was a young African-American girl. She had been sitting on a rickety chair while she drew in a little notebook.

"I asked, who are you?"

"I'm...ah, Chase."

She continued to eye him up and down. Her stare was ominous. He took a step back. She gave him a look like that was a smart move.

"I'm Maddy." Then quickly returned to her investigation, "Why are you dressed like that?"

"I was just in Greece."

"You were just in Greece?"

"Yeah."

"And people in Greece dress like that?"

"Well, no. I mean they used to."

"They used to?"

"Yeah."

"But they don't anymore?"

"I don't know."

"Then why'd you say they do."

Chase was at a loss of words.

"You don't have anything else to wear?"

"Yeah, I do."

Chase came out of the tool shed wearing his 21st century clothes. Maddy, however, had a new opinion for Chase, "That's better?"

Chase checked himself out. He found no fault in his look. Besides, he had no time for the hassle. He had to find the portal.

"What time is it?"

She checked out the sun, squinted and reasonably determined, "11:37."

Chase was amazed…and slightly confused. Then, Maddy revealed she was joking, "Nah, but it feels like twenty minutes until lunch."

"No, I meant 'what is the year and the date?'"

"You don't know the year?"

"No. I've been in Greece…and they use a different calendar."

"Maybe that's why they aren't the greatest civilization anymore."

Chase's eyes showed he was not in the mood.

"It's 1896."

"1896…and where are we?"

"West Orange."

"West Orange?"

"Yeah."

"In Jersey?"

"Yes, Jersey."

"Is this place some kind of hideout for the government?"

"No. Why would you say that?"

"All the lab coats in there. When I came in, they chased me out like I was going to see some big government secret. It was just a little weird."

"Big secrets, yes. Government, no."

"So where am I?"

"You are at the home of the world's greatest inventor."

"Who is…?"

Now Maddy's eyes show she's in disbelief. "Thomas Edison."

"Oh…" Chase knew about Edison. He'd heard about him. A lot. He almost came to this place on a class field trip but he was sick with the flu that day. He started to peek around the corner when the door to the large black barn opened and the lab coats filed out like a military regiment. Chase ducked back behind the edge of the barn. He didn't need any more hassle for the moment.

As he hid, Maddy barreled ahead. Her focus was the last man in the line…and the only one not wearing a lab coat. He was shorter than most and in a brown tweed suit. The kind that a professor in college would wear.

And from the tattered looks of it, he did…twenty years ago. The elbows were worn and the knees dirty, the suit looked like it had "been lived in" for quite some time.

Maddy could care less about the clothes the man wore, she was concerned with his latest contraption.

"Mr. Edison, can I please see the projector after lunch?"

"Miss Taylor, how do you know what we have inside Black Maria?"

Now Maddy was battling nerves. She trailed Edison like the idol she knew he was. Edison continued to pepper her with questions, "Was that boy one of your spies? WAS HE?"

"No, Mr. Edison. No! He was not with me."

Edison had stopped and gave Maddy a very serious scowl. His eyes only drifted up and over her shoulder when Chase peeked around the corner once more. "He sure looks like he's with you!"

Maddy glanced over her shoulder with a bigger scowl than Thomas Edison. "HE'S NOT WITH ME!"

"No matter. This is not a good time. We are in a tricky little negotiation at the moment. If things get done this afternoon, maybe I can show you something later this evening. Now run along and get back to school."

"Yes, sir."

Edison turned and made his way in the same direction as the rest of the scientists. Maddy knew that was the kitchen. And a big lunch. She let him get out of sight before she doubled back to the large black barn they had named Black Maria. She approached the door.

A moment of thought and decision and another glance over her shoulder.

She slowly cracked the door open. Then, she quickly disappeared inside. Chase, still hiding around the side of the structure, also decided to move. He was compelled to see what Maddy saw…or wanted to see. He took the twenty or so steps to the door, cracked it open and slid inside.

Pitch black once more. And no beam of light hitting him in the face. But also no sound. Whatsoever. Pitch black and completely quiet. Eerie quiet. Then it hit him, *was he in some portal middle ground? Did he just make another jump and didn't realize it? Was that all his time with Mr. Edison? What was happening? Usually, his time jumps were so quick. He walked through the door and he shot into another time and place. Instantly. Boom. No time to think. Just time to react…hopefully. But this time…nothing. Nothing at all. No light. No sound. No clue.*

"BOO!" Chase leapt straight out of his underwear. His heart raced. His palms sweat. His lungs gasped for air. Maddy was standing right behind him. And she was giggling.

"Why'd you do that?!"

"Why'd you follow me?"

Chase didn't have an answer. He couldn't really tell her the whole deal with the portals or anything. He didn't really know her and maybe she didn't really need to know. So he just shrugged his shoulders.

"Huh?" She couldn't see his shoulders so she didn't know he had responded to her question.

He finally added, "I don't know. Geez…"

Maddy wasn't behind Chase anymore. He could tell that because across the room, a small light flicked on.

She was fifteen feet away and checking out the object of focus and desire this afternoon. Chase crept a few cautious steps toward her and the machine. He could tell from the lens that it was the machine that shot light directly into his eyes earlier. And when he began to circle the contraption, he could tell it was some old looking movie projector. What he couldn't tell or hadn't figured out, was that it was the first real movie projector ever created. And what he also couldn't tell was that he was staring at a piece of history that would change the world. He'd later tell anyone who asked, "I mean, c'mon, I was twelve when I saw it. I can't know everything!"

"Isn't it beautiful?" He noticed Maddy and the absolute rapt attention she was paying it. Chase said he guessed so.

"No, I mean, how amazing is it that it will project moving images on the wall."

Again, this was not so amazing for Chase Axelrod of the 21st century. He'd been to countless movies. And movies that were a little more than the black and white images she was talking about.

"I think…" Maddy flipped a switch and then another.

"What are you doing?"

"Trying to get this thing to work."

"Aren't you going to get in trouble?"

"Not if they don't catch me."

Chase didn't care to stick around. He was sure he would not be impressed. And he was quite sure he didn't need any more trouble. Thus he made his way out of the lab room.

He'd spotted a back door and made his way toward it. It did not lead outside, however but into a smaller back room that looked very much like a storage facility. He stood at the door way and took in the different machines and devices.

From what he could tell, he recognized an old record player, kind of like the one he'd seen at Grandpa Wally's. He spotted more light bulbs of various shapes and sizes. Then his eyes caught a machine that had thin tape coming out of it. It sat silent at the moment but from what he could tell, the tape moved from a roll, through the machine and out the other side.

"It's a stock ticker. Now get over here and help me thread this film through the machine."

Maddy had a way of taking charge and Chase had a way of listening to her. She did like this about Chase. Probably the only thing she liked about him at this exact minute.

She dragged him over to the projector and ordered him to push the film back through the slot in an even and steady pace. Chase did as he was told until the film began to back up and got caught on one of the gears.

"Where's the holes?"

Maddy stared at him like he was crazy.

"You know, the little holes on each side of the film?"

Maddy had no clue as to what he was saying.

"The film is supposed to have little holes on each side so it catches and feeds through and doesn't get stuck in the machine."

His idea intrigued her and her face showed it. Chase continued, "If the film sits in one place too long, it will melt from the heat of the bulb. You can't let it get caught or you need to turn it off quickly. That seems to be the problem here."

Maddy's eyes went from Chase to the projector and back to Chase. Then they squinted. "Are you trying to take my place?"

Chase had no idea what she was talking about so he just stared blankly.

"Are you? Are you trying to become an inventor? Is that why you showed up here?! Are you moving in on my turf like a slippery snake?"

"No."

"Huh? Is that why you're here?"

"No."

"Cause we're going to have a big problem if Mr. Edison takes you on and leaves me behind."

"No. That's not what—"

"—oh, I will knock you out if you try to weasel in on my place. I've been here everyday for the last eight months waiting for my chance to join his team."

"I don't want to join his team."

Maddy kept ranting so Chase finally interrupted at the top of his lungs. "I DON'T WANT TO WORK WITH THOMAS EDISON!"

"Why not? Am I that bad?" The two kids whipped their heads around to see the small man in the open doorway. They both cowered at the same time. Caught. Red-handed. And now they both knew what was coming: punishment.

"I'm sorry, Mr. Edison."

"Yeah, I'm sorry too."

"Sorry doesn't help me fix this machine. It was broken before and now it's really screwed up. And I just had an ad placed in the paper that says we are behind schedule."

Edison held up a copy of the New York Times. He pointed to a small advertisement, mixed in with dozens of other theatre ads that read:

KOSTER AND BIAL'S MUSIC HALL, 34th St.
TOMORROW (MONDAY) NIGHT.
THE ONLY CHEVALIER CANCELLED for the first
public exhibition of Edison's latest marvel,
THE VITASCOPE.

"Now, get out of my laboratory so I can get to work and fix this god-forsaken machine."

The rest of the white coats shuffled into the room as the two kids were ushered out.

"Mr. Edison, I think we can help you fix that."

"Maddy, I've had enough distractions today."

"But Mr. Edison!"

"MADDY! Enough."

They were standing outside, when they looked back to see the door being shut on them. For some reason, Chase felt compelled to yell, "HOLES! HOLES IN THE FILM!" The door was latched shut. They heard the lock turning. They would not be getting back inside anytime soon.

"So what now?"

Maddy knew, "Follow me."

She led him to the back of the large red house. She popped up the steps that lead to the kitchen and in through the screen door. She acted like she owned the place, grabbing a few buttermilk biscuits and an apple. She tossed Chase half of her take. He seemed grateful. It had been a while since he had eaten. And as quick as she has entered, she was back out the door. It was a quick hit and run. Chase inhaled his biscuit and grabbed another for good measure before he ran to catch up with his new friend.

By the time Maddy actually stopped, she was out by a small brook in the middle of the forest. It was a very quiet and peaceful little place amongst a shady grove of trees. Maddy seemed to be half happy, half-annoyed that she had a shadow this afternoon.

"I'm going to be here a while."

Chase nodded.

"And I'm not going to be talking."

Chase nodded again.

She reached into the side pocket of her dress and pulled out her folded notebook. From the other side pocket, she produced a stub of a pencil. Chase watched as she opened the notebook to find the next blank page. He continued to peer over her shoulder as she sketched an exact copy of the film projector she saw only a few minutes ago. Her drawing didn't just include the projector itself. It also included the darkness around it. She shaded the background and the way the light hit its side. It was a spot on duplicate of Edison's newest toy.

When she was finished, she looked at Chase for approval or praise. He nodded again. She could tell he was impressed. Then he pulled off his backpack and dug out the Faber Castell Polychromos artist grade colored pencils. As he offered, her face quickly showed a sense of awe. It took her a few minutes to pull the first pencil out of the small wooden case. The colors, so vivid. The pencil was long and nearly new. The points sharpened perfectly. The decision was almost too much.

Finally, the dark green slid out of the case and into her hand. She slowly began the process of drawing a new vision. The grove in which they stood now became her scene. Chase fashioned himself an artist. And he was good, but nothing like Maddy. She could take a glance at something and draw it from memory. Chase was good but much more methodical. Good, detailed but slow. Or slower.

When it came to Maddy the artist, he was impressed. Really impressed. He knew he was in the presence of a great artist. And he tried to sneak a peek or two...or three.

As focused as she would get into her work, she could feel his hovering over her shoulder. And it annoyed her. Without looking up, without moving and without stopping, she grumbled, "STOP!"

Chase took a step back. And he tried to get back to his own work, but his eyes couldn't help but drift to her notebook again. And so he shifted a little. And nudged a half-a-squirm closer. He craned his neck higher just to catch a glimpse.

"I said STOP."

"Why are you so mad at me?"

Chase's question made Maddy stop. She stared at him.

"I asked you why you are so mad at me."

"You're trying to take what's mine."

"No I'm not."

"Yes, you are. I can see it."

"I don't know what you're talking about. I don't want anything that's yours."

"Oh no?!" She turned her body to face Chase. And stood now. She was about to make a point. "You didn't just appear at the home of Thomas Edison?"

Chase guessed that was true.

"And you didn't just come up with a solution to his next great invention?"

"I...I...guess. But I've seen those before."

With a laser-like mind, she jumped on his words, "Really!?" 'I've seen it before.' So, you're here to help the man and then he'll like you and hire you to be his assistant when I've been waiting outside his lab for almost a year! And you don't think you're trying to take what's mine?!"

"I'm not. I'm really not. I just want to figure out why I'm here and then get back home. Really. That's all I want."

Maddy was quiet but her face showed she was unconvinced.

"I don't want to be Thomas Edison's assistant. I don't want to be an inventor and I don't want to stay in New Jersey."

"OK."

Now Chase was unconvinced. "OK, you believe me?"

"Shouldn't I?"

"Yes. You should. I just don't believe it."

She asked why.

"Because you've been mean to me since I got here and I still think you're going to be mean again. You've got this look like you want to kill me. Geez..."

"I'm not mean. I'm black. And a girl."

Chase was totally confused now. "What's that got to do with anything? I go to school with lots of black girls. They aren't mean to me. We're friends. I mean I think we are. We talk and laugh and joke and study and—"

"Well your home sounds great but where I live, we don't get chances like this. We don't get to learn from great inventors like Mr. Edison. Most white men don't even give me the time of day."

Chase had no idea what to say so he just said the first thing that came to mind. "I gave you my favorite pencils. That's something."

Maddy looked at him. She believed he did. And she believed, that <u>was</u> something. "Thanks."

"You're welcome."

As night fell, the kids returned to the house. The grounds shimmered in all the lights. As they neared the house Edison called Glenmont, Chase could tell the man who perfected the light bulb lived here. Much different from the other houses in the surrounding area. Once their eyes adjusted from the glimmering house, Maddy glanced at the large black barn that housed the film projector. She focused on the small light peeking out from the cracks of the laboratory. With her inquisitive mind, there was only one thing to do.

Edison was putzing with the projector when the kids entered. Or he was. He had fallen asleep near the contraption, his head leaning against the side of it. The footsteps of Chase and Maddy had jostled him awake.

"Holes."

Edison looked at her.

"Holes. Little ones in the film."

The great inventor was intrigued. So he asked for more…but Maddy didn't have any more than that.

Chase chimed in to save his friend, "Along the edge. She means holes along the edge that could catch on a gear and feed the film through and not get jammed."

Edison appreciated a good idea. "That could work. It would take too long to make it work for the first exhibition but I like that for the future. Good job, Maddy."

"I can help you, Mr. Edison."

"Yeah…" Edison didn't believe her.

"I can."

"Settle down, Maddy. Settle down. You had a good idea. Let's just leave it at that."

"Is this because I'm a girl?"

"No, because most people who approach me aren't for real. They take a short cut. How do I know that the idea is not the boy's? How do I know that you just took his idea and made it your own?"

"Like you did today?"

Edison's eyebrow rose.

"You just bought that guy's projector and named it for your own."

She was right. And Edison knew it.

"Right?" She continued making her point. Edison was quiet. "So you just took his idea and made it your own."

"I've earned that right."

"Just because you have money? That's why?"

"I have the right to do that because I created…the stock ticker, the incandescent bulb, the phonograph…and I invented something like it called the kinetoscope. Plus, I'm going to make it better."

"But you didn't invent it."

"But I'm going to make it better."

"It's Edison in name only." Maddy walked over to Edison's desk. She began reading from a placard he had placed there many years ago. It was a quote from Sir Joshua Reynolds: *'There is no expedient to which a man will not resort to avoid the real labor of thinking.'* I've seen this slogan displayed in other places around here, haven't I?"

He grew tired of arguing with her. "If you stop, I'll take you to the exhibition."

Maddy had gotten her way. She'd take that deal.

"Hey Chase, you ever been to New York City?"

Chapter 8

"I'm going home?"

A huge smiled appeared on Chase's face. New York City. Awesome! Maybe the portal would be in his house. And he could just be back at home in the present day and he could sleep in his own bed and be done with all this hassle.

"Be here at 8 AM sharp!" Edison bellowed.

They both nodded.

"Now get out of here. I need to be alone."

They both nodded again before leaving the lab.

Outside Maddy began heading home, "So I will see you tomorrow morning."

Chase nodded.

When she turned around, Chase hadn't moved. "Where you sleeping tonight?"

Chase shrugged.

"You ever been to the ghetto?"

Chase shook his head no.

"C'mon. I'll protect you." Then she added, "But keep your mouth shut and your head down."

That scared Chase a little.

They came to a stop a half a mile down the road. From atop a small bluff, a collection of shacks appeared below in a valley. This "village" had sprung up in no defined order around the small pond that edged most of the homes. A few candles burned in the windows but for the most part, the homes were dark. Not just the tar-paper that covered their wooden slats and made up the sides and roofs, but inside as well. Chase could smell the small fireplaces burning wood and cooking dinners.

Maddy strolled down the main dirt road to the third house on the left. Her hand pressed against Chase chest, motioning him to stop. "Wait here."

She bounced up the single step and inside the shack. The thin wood door swung wide-open then back but not quite closed. Still ajar, Chase could see the events occurring inside. Maddy had dropped her notebook on the rickety kitchen table as she entered and kissed her mother on the cheek. Without hearing what was being said, anyone could tell a sales job was going on.

She had turned on the charm. But her mother, who had probably seen this act a hundred times, was not entertained. Especially when she looked up and out the door. Her eyes made contact with Chase and her look was not welcoming.

At that moment, Chase knew this was going to be a long night. Her glare continued, so he moved out of sight line. He began kicking the stones in the road, fiddling with his backpack and anything else to pass the time. He looked around at the other homes. And the other homes looked back at him. At least the owners and residents of those homes. Chase was getting the feeling that not too many white people were seen in this neighborhood.

"You telling my girl you don't have a home?!"

Chase whipped his head around to see Maddy's mother on the step of her house. The entire neighborhood was staring at Chase. He barely eked out a yes.

"You got to be kidding me. Where's your Momma?"

Sheepishly, Chase answered, "ah…Minnesota…at the moment."

"Where?!"

Maddy felt compelled to add, "Minnesota, Momma. It's a state in the Midwest."

"Then why ain't you with her?!"

Chase didn't have the answer. Or really the time or inclination to answer that question truthfully so he just shrugged his shoulders.

Maddy's Mother could only shake her head at the lack of answers out of this boy. "You can sleep on the porch." She turned to go inside and as she did, she began to mumble under her breath, "Crazy white folk make no sense…"

Maddy stood still, staring at Chase. "She'll let you sleep out here." Maddy pointed to the three-foot wide porch facing the road. It was covered with a small awning. As Chase sat down and looked up, he was grateful the sky was full of stars and not rain clouds.

From inside, "MADELINE, GET IN HERE!"

Maddy sprinted through the door.

Chase was all alone. He grabbed his sweatshirt out of his backpack and put it on. He sat down, putting his back against the side of Maddy's home. He scanned the surroundings. A number of neighbors still glared at him as though he was right out of the circus. He tried to ignore them but their looks were filled with uncomfortable unease.

Thirty minutes later, Maddy snuck out of the shack, careful to not let the door squeak when it opened or slam when it closed. In her hand, she carried a small clay bowl that contained some steaming gumbo. She handed it to him.

Chase held it like the most precious thing he'd ever handled. The heat from the contents warmed his hands. The night air had cooled and chilled Chase. This offering from his friend was very welcome. He brought the bowl to his lips and began to sip the warm stew into his belly. He was instantly ten degrees warmer and twenty degrees happier.

Maddy whispered. "You have to understand that my Momma's from Alabama. And down there, they don't get along too well with white folk."

Chase nodded.

"It's not that she doesn't like you. It's not that at all."

"Sure felt like that."

"It's not that. It's that she doesn't understand you."

"What's not to understand?"

"Why you hate us so much?"

"I don't hate—"

"—white people. Why whites hate blacks?"

"I don't hate blacks."

"You might not but your people sure do."

"Not my people!"

"You're not white?!" She started laughing when she said that.

"No. I'm white! I just meant my people don't hate black people."

"Well, your people have a funny way of showing it."

Chase was at a loss. He didn't understand. He didn't know what to say. And his brain had kicked into overdrive to try to do either...or both.

"Maddy, I don't hate black people. Some of my friends are black. I like hip-hop. And rap. I like Jay-Z. I like Kanye. I go to school with black people and I—"

Maddy started laughing. She tried to suppress it to a giggle but she couldn't help it.

"What?"

"You go to school with black people. You said you go to school with black people."

"I did. I do!"

"That's funny, white boy. That's funny."

"I do!"

"That's impossible."

"What?"

"MADELINE, DON'T TELL ME YOU'RE OUT ON THAT PORCH!"

Maddy almost jumped out of her clothes before she again sprinted inside. "See you tomorrow."

Chase finally fell asleep. It took some time. He was scared. He didn't feel welcome. He thought someone may approach and give him problems. And when that didn't happen, he began to hear all the sounds of the countryside. The owls hooting. The coyotes howling. The raccoons prowling. The sounds that only happen in the dark, dark, countryside. The kinds of sounds that you don't hear in the city of New York. The sounds of animals…scary ones…moving around at night. In the darkness. And the sounds that get louder as they get closer and closer and sometimes their eyes open only a few feet away from yours. And sometimes the moon shines just bright enough to see the white and black stripes of a very smelly skunk. It's the sights and sounds that kept a young boy awake. Wide awake. And nervous. And tense. And, if he had to admit it, a little bit scared.

When his eyelids finally got too heavy and he drifted off to sleep, Chase did get some rest. Not enough and not good sleep, but it was something. Of course, there was something very unsettling when one gets awakened in a jarring manner. Or by a stranger that sets your nerves off like a firecracker screaming into the sky. That's what happened to Chase.

He wasn't jarred from his sleep. No, the person waking him was very gentle and his voice was deep and low. And not scary. Well, not until Chase opened his eyes and saw an elderly black man inches from his face. Chase twitched and flinched and scrambled backward, pressing his head and back against the wall of the house.

"Now, now son. I'm not going to hurt you. Not going to hurt you at all." The soothing voice came from an old man with a big, gentle smile and kind eyes. Chase stopped his threshing. He sat still and he listened.

"There you go. Right as rain, I won't hurt you none."

The gentleman offered Chase a bowl similar to the one Maddy brought him last night. As Chase peered inside, he saw a white, oatmeal looking mixture. He grabbed the bowl. Again, it was warm. He held it longer than he should but his hands were quite cold and the bowl felt great.

"Go on. Take it in. Grits is a good start for a long day."

Chase began to sip and swallow the grits and while the taste wasn't in his top ten, he was in no position to argue or complain.

"There you go. You eat them grits and you'll have the best day you've had in a long time."

Chase continued to eat as the old man sat in a chair next to him.

"Son, what brings you to my home?"

Chase had a mouthful so he couldn't answer.

"Maddy says you work with Mr. Edison."

"Sort of."

"Sort of? Either you do or you don't. Which is it?"

"I guess I am at the moment."

The old man thought for a moment before asking, "Maddy says she works with him too. Is that true?"

"From what I can see."

"Well...how about that...never thought I'd ever see that."

"What's that, sir? What didn't you think you'd see?"

"My granddaughter working with Mr. Edison."

"Why?"

"When we work with men like that, we usually cleaning and cooking and the like."

"That's all?"

"That's all." The old man chuckled. "That's pretty good, young man. Working honest is working well. Doing the Lord's tasks." The old man glanced down at Chase and an empty bowl of grits. "Like the work you did on them grits."

Chase looked down at the empty bowl and then up at the old man with a big smile.

"I want to apologize 'bout my family's hospitality. If I would have known you were here, I would have given you my bed."

Chase was silent. He didn't know what to say.

"I'm sorry you had to sleep out here. And you must forgive my daughter. It won't happen again as long as I'm taking breaths."

Again, he didn't know what to say.

"I hope it wasn't too bad for ya."

"It was a little creepy."

"The critters?"

"Yeah…" Chase shouldn't say it but he liked the old man and felt he could share a little more. "…and your neighbors."

"Oh yeah?"

"Yeah. I got some mean looks."

"Sounds about right."

"It does?"

"They don't really like your kind."

"But I didn't do anything to them."

"Maybe not you. But they been getting put down by white people for as long as they remember. And their mommas and daddies have been seeing it for as long as they can remember. It's just the way this world works."

"It doesn't have to work that way."

The old man chuckled. "Sure, son. Sure it don't, but that what it does."

"It's not that way where I live."

"There ain't no blacks where you come from?"

"No, there are blacks."

"But you white people are just so nice that we all live together, happy and free?"

"Well…" Chase didn't really know how to answer that.

"Son, I was born into slavery. Down in Alabama. I was not free. And I was not counted as a man. Nope. I was three-fifths. Three-fifths a person. And I never got to say how my life was going to be. I had some white man telling me. Told me when to eat. When to sleep. When to work and when to stop. And this had been happening to my daddy and his daddy and his. And all these people you saw last night had the same life. So when we got the chance, we left. Just like the rest of these people. My family came north because we thought it could be better."

"And it's not?"

"Son, what I've learned is racism is everywhere. Just because the state says a man is free, don't mean he is."

"But nobody owns you, right?"

"The system does. I can't vote. Maddy can't go to the same school you can. I don't go to the same market as Mr. Edison. Can't even live in the same neighborhood."

"But..." Chase was flustered and confused but the old man looked like he was done talking about it so he just changed the subject. "Heard you going into the city today."

"Yes. Sir."

"You promise me something."

Chase listened.

"You promise me you keep my little Maddy out of trouble."

Chase agreed.

"God knows I would try to talk her out of going but that would be as useless as selling sand to a sailor. So I won't try. New York scares me. Lots of trouble for a young girl out there. But it wouldn't be no good for a Grandpa to tell his granddaughter she can't do something when she's got her mind set." He paused, looking at Chase solemnly, "But I can ask her friend to protect her, can't I?"

"Yes. Yes, you can. And yes. Yes, I will."

The old man held out his hand to shake Chase's. Chase complied.

"Thank you…"

"Chase. My name is Chase."

"Nice to meet you Chase. My name is Wallace."

Chase's eyes widened, "That's my grandpa's name."

"Then he must be a good man."

"He is."

"And I bet you love him."

Chase nodded.

"Then tell him that the next time you see him. It will make his day."

Maddy bolted out of the house, "Grandpa, what are you doing?"

"I was just introducing myself to your friend Chase."

"My friend?"

"Oh Maddy. Don't be like your mother. You don't have to be so tough. You wouldn't have brought him here if you didn't like him."

Maddy rolled her eyes before announcing that Chase and her needed to get going. "Can't be late!"

The horses neighed and whinnied as the kids loaded themselves into the wagon that held the Vitascope. Renamed with Edison's brand and approval, tonight the exhibition would bring motion pictures to a mainstream audience.

Three "lab coats" had tied down the machine but Edison was taking nothing for granted. They all rode with at least a hand on the projector. One of them would go down before his contraption.

The horse driver let out a whistle and a big "YAAHHH!" The caravan of wagons slowly began to move forward. *"NEXT STOP, NEW YORK CITY!"*

Chapter 9

"Next stop, New York City..."

Those words echoed inside Chase's brain. *Boy, that sounded good, he thought.*

He was about to be disappointed. The New York City that came into view was a far cry from the one in which he lived. The ferry across the Hudson River was the first sign. No George Washington Bridge or Holland Tunnel. Then, he passed a Statue of Liberty that looked copper and not green.

As the boat pulled up to the pier, the same glorious skyscrapers he was used to seeing weren't there. Neither was the Empire State Building. Nor the Chrysler Building. In fact, Manhattan of 1896 looked more like Brooklyn of the twenty-first century. The city he saw may have been called New York, but it wasn't home.

Maddy must have read it on Chase's face. "Something wrong?"

"It's different."

"Really? How long have you been gone?"

Chase had to think...then he realized he'd be counting forward. In his head, he did the math. The correct answer would be -114 years. He decided to just swallow that answer. "Awhile."

A deck hand reached out to pull the kids up from the ferry deck as Maddy's questioning continued, "How long is awhile?"

"Ah...a year."

"Oh." She seemed to accept that answer before her eyes moved from interrogating Chase and onto the city in front of her. "WOWWWWW!"

Chase stopped to look again. It wasn't his New York...but I guess it had to start somewhere. When he gazed again, it started to grab him a little more. Then he looked down. Not to the cobblestone streets, but to the sidewalks.

New York was moving. And moving in a hurry! Now that part of New York City was the same. *Maybe this wouldn't be so bad.* The wagons disembarked from the ferry and were rolling down the streets in no time.

When Edison's caravan came to a stop, they were in front of the Koster and Bial's Music Hall. The marquee was beaming. It read: **TONIGHT: Edison's Vitascope. Pictures in motion! First theatrical exhibition!**

Something about this area looked familiar to Chase and his curiosity prompted him to ask, "Where are we?"

"Koster and Bial."

"No," Chase scoffed. "What street is this?"

"34th and Broadway."

"34th and Broadway?! That sounded familiar. "Wait, isn't that Macy's?" It was…or would be. In the twentieth century. But that will be six years from now.

"Nope. Macy's is on 18th and Broadway."

The crew unloaded the projector at a slow and steady pace. Mr. Edison hawked and hovered over every move. A protective father, he surely was but the workers seemed used to his shouts and directions. They quietly lifted and shifted, nudged and noodled the entire contraption through the door and up the winding stairs to the balcony.

Chase and Maddy attempted to make themselves useful but they were no help. They both knew the scowl on Mr. Edison's face meant they should steer clear.

"You're lucky just to be here." They needed to be silent shadows for the rest of the day.

The first glitch in the projector move occurred when it did not quite fit the stairwell turn. The group was at an impasse. About this time, the manager of the theatre tapped Edison's shoulder, asking for a moment of his time. He whispered in Mr. Edison's ear, while pointing at Maddy and Chase. Clearly angry, Edison barked something back in his ear and the manager quickly ran off, but not without a crusty look for Maddy.

The men circled up like a football team in a huddle. Everyone offered ideas but Edison was the undisputed quarterback. After lots of thought and suggestions, the group decided to take one piece carefully off the machine and transport the projector around the curves in two pieces.

"You'll break it and we'll never get it fixed in time for the show!" Edison wasn't on board…until they began to talk to the engineering side of his brain.

"Three quick bolts. Three more screws. None of the guts of the machine would be disturbed." That is what the team told Edison.

Maddy tugged on the sleeve of Edison's topcoat. She had another idea. It was never heard.

"Not now, Madeline. Not now." She sulked off and Edison finally nodded his approval. The team began to break it down.

The projector was still being worked on, when the manager returned minutes later. Again, he whispered to Edison. This time he was far more animated. He kept saying something about his boss not standing for something. The only line Chase could make out was, "It's just unacceptable! Just unacceptable!" From the look on Edison's face, his nerves were wearing thin.

As this was going on a few feet away, Maddy had jumped in, holding a small wrench and a few screws. She was doing her best to help the white coats out. This was not going to be her finest moment. In an exchange from one of the lab coats, a small screw accidentally fell out of her hand, bounced on the floor and slid into a small air grate in the floor. Gone forever.

Edison hadn't really been listening to the theatre manager. He had been watching his team. And he had seen the screw's fateful fall at the same moment the manager really raised his voice, "She's colored and she can't be in here!"

Edison snapped. He barked at Maddy. "Make yourself useful…outside!"

She could tell she was not wanted at the moment. Her head dropped and she shuffled out. A hand appeared on her shoulder. It was the theatre manager. He was smiling as he began to guide her out of the main room. Another hand pulled his hand. It was the hand of Edison.

"Remove your hand right now." Edison's voice was forceful. The manager did not argue. He simply and quickly walked away.

Edison knelt down. "I'm sorry, Madeline."

Tears had welled up in her eyes.

"Could you do me a favor and make sure our wagons are doing fine?"

She nodded, but wouldn't look him in the face.

"You will be in here tonight. I promise. You'll be right next to me."

That promise proved a little more successful as a small smile formed on her face. She turned and left. Chase watched her slow and sad exit before looking back to Edison. He asked with his eyes and shoulders if he could join Maddy outside and Edison quickly agreed.

Chase came out of the theatre to see Maddy sitting on the front bench of the first wagon crying. He hopped up to the shotgun seat and started rubbing her back. "That was horrible."

Maddy said nothing.

"I can't believe that happened in New York."

Maddy looked Chase in the eyes. She shook her head at his ignorance.

"So, should we feed the horses?"

She was not here for that. "I'm not a stable hand! _We_ can do more than serve food to the animals!"

Uncomfortable, Chase's eyes darted to a random man standing next to them on the sidewalk.

"Sir, which way to 101st and Broadway?

The man chuckled, "101st? There is no 101st."

"What?"

"Don't mock your elders, son!"

Chase knew there was...or would be so he really wasn't mocking him. He covered rapidly, "Which way to Central Park?"

The man pointed behind them. Then asked, "Shouldn't little urchins like you be in school instead of telling jokes?"

Chase ignored the man and turned to Maddy, "If you don't feed them, maybe you can steer them."

She didn't know what Chase meant until he let out a huge "YEEHHAWW!" The horses snapped to attention and began moving...actually trotting. Quickly, it was nearing a gallop. Maddy dove for the reins. She snagged one but the other fell off the footboard. Luckily for her...and Chase, it was the right rein. She pulled with all her might and turned these horses 180 degrees around like a pro.

Maddy turned them but she didn't stop them. They were still off and galloping. The streets seemed to corral the horses from going too off course. They stayed on the street. Maintaining a brisk pace, Maddy and Chase were heading in the direction of Central Park.

As the wagon headed north on Broadway, the various sections of Manhattan passed. The Garment District. Times Square. The Theatre District. And finally Central Park.

It wasn't the same park that Chase had run through, played in and where he had hit baseballs with his dad. First of all, no hot dog vendors. Or paved sidewalks. No Tavern on the Green. And no baseball diamonds.

Actually, Central Park looked horrible. The weeds around the paths were knee high. Trash was blowing through the fields. It looked like no one but the farm animals were caring for Chase's favorite playground.

Wait, farm animals? Chase did a double take. There were SHEEP grazing throughout the park! The grass in the middle of the park looked mowed. Except it wasn't mowed…it was eaten…by the sheep were grazing in the middle of Central Park! Just another sign that Chase's neighborhood would not be the same.

But there was no time to wallow, the wagon kept moving. And very fast at that. Chase kept looking over at Maddy, wondering if she really had control of the horses. He pointed to the left, directing Maddy to turn. She pulled the reins and the wagon did turn but at that speed, the wagon went up on two wheels.

Their eyes went wide open. All four of them. This was a real-life roller coaster. The wagon teetered as the horses barreled forward. Thanks to a rut in the dirt road that caused the wheels to tilted back to normal. Chase and Maddy were safe…or safer. Of course, the horses still ran.

The wagon rumbled quickly past Central Park. And the kids began to recover their wits….not all of them but the ride seemed to be getting a little smoother.

"Are we OK?"

Maddy turned her head toward Chase and tried to smile. At that moment, the wagon hit a pothole. It sent them flying upward and then gravity kicked in and their backsides came down just as fast. BOOM…both were instantly hurting.

"Oh, my tailbone!"

But they had no time to whine. The wagon was again gaining more speed. It was actually reaching its limit. To add to the peril, the street was littered with people and animals. Maddy tried her best to weave through the obstacles in the street. They narrowly missed pedestrians, other wagons and dogs and children and anything else that seemed to cross in front of them…which at the moment seemed to be all of New York.

"Help me, Chase!"

He tried. He grabbed onto the reins with Maddy. They both pulled and pulled but the horses did not seem to care. They were spooked. And they were running. Only mother-nature and exhaustion would calm these huge animals.

Over the noises of the creaks and the bouncing, the wagon felt like it would crash or fall apart at any moment. Nobody knew which would happen first!

"Just work with me." Chase was holding the right rein and pushing the left one toward Maddy. "Steer until they get tired!" She heard Chase's shouts and nodded in agreement.

For the next five minutes, they leaned and pulled and kept the wagon upright and straight. With a little skill and lots of luck, they avoided all the possible accidents that appeared. Partly, because they had the horses running through the park.

Finally, the horses began to tire. They slowed and slowed, moving from a gallop to a trot. The kids pulled back again and this time they were successful. The horses obeyed their drivers and came to a stop.

The kids bolted from the wagon. Nothing could keep Maddy and Chase on that wagon any longer. If the horses ran off, so be it. At that moment, they didn't care.

"Where are we?"

Chase tried to get his bearings. To his right, was most of Central Park. But he couldn't really gather his location because there were hardly any landmarks. He knew New York by the buildings. And the subway stations. And the smells. The pizza on the corner. The Chinese restaurant four blocks up from his apartment. The hot dog cart by Lincoln Center.

That's how he knew the city. He could walk without looking. He just knew where to turn by smell. He usually went to school…or his friend's house on autopilot. And it was good for Chase to perfect this process because most of the time his nose was stuck in his Nintendo DS. The only world he'd conquered were won by jumping dragons and avoiding fireballs.

So when Maddy again asked where they were, Chase's brain went into double time. "Lemme see…"

"I thought this was your home!"

"It will be."

"Huh?"

He let it slip. "Nothing! Mind your own business!"

"C'mon." Chase started walking. Toward the setting sun. And Maddy followed. They got back to Central Park West when a building finally popped in Chase's eyes. It was so distinct in its architecture and one of only two completed buildings on the street and a few hundred feet away that it couldn't help but stand out.

The rest of the smaller houses were in various stages of construction but this building dominated the street. It looked kinda like a castle. At least that's what Chase always thought. His Dad had showed him the building many years ago and told him that a very famous man had been shot here before he was born. Some guy in a band.

The kids strolled toward it.

Maddy read the post box. "Says here it's call The Dakota."

"Our apartment is just a few blocks from here."

Maddy was excited, "Let's go see it!"

Chase and Maddy turned down the street. One block later, there were no buildings nearby. Two blocks later, just fields of shrubs and brush. Three blocks, more fields and a lot of wonder.

"You said a few blocks?"

Chase stared...in astonishment. He could see where his building was or would be, but as of right now, it was a field of dirt, a few trees and a few more puddles.

Chase couldn't believe it. His building didn't exist. *When do they build it? When will they make my room?*

"Are you sure you're not crazy?" Maddy asked.

Chase stared straight ahead.

"Chase?"

"They'll build it. In the future."

"You know, you seem to think you know a lot of what's _going_ to happen."

"I do."

"Why?"

"Cause that's where I'm from."

Maddy smiled at Chase's wacky statement. But Chase didn't smile back. Then she giggled. He didn't. He was still stunned from his home not existing. That got Maddy thinking.

"Are you really telling me you are from the future?"

That snapped Chase out of his trance. "No. Why?"

"I'm just joking...but you just sounded so serious."

"Let's get back to the theatre."

Maddy agreed and they headed off back to the horses.

A few quiet steps and Maddy had another question. A big one! "Are you and Edison creating a time machine?"

Chase's eyes popped open. "WHAT?"

Maddy was again joking but Chase's response caused her to rethink that. "You are, aren't you!? That's why you just appeared. And that's why he's been so quiet about you and never mentioned you and invited you along to the picture show. That's it! If Thomas Edison has a time machine, he's going to be richer than rich."

"He doesn't have a time machine."

"He could."

"Nope."

"How do you know?! He's the greatest inventor ever. And he's the smartest man ever!"

"No, he's not!"

"Who's smarter?" she asked.

"Einstein."

"Who's Einstein?"

"Never mind. We're late."

They rushed back to the theatre. With the horses. But this time, they kept control of the wagon. As they ducked in the back door, Chase led. Maddy told him he had to. That way she could sneak by the theatre manager. By the time they got to Edison, the film was wrapping up. Chase watched as much as he could, but he was unimpressed. *Wait 'til they see Star Wars or Jurassic Park or Lord of the Rings. This was nothing.* And Chase wanted to say something but he remembered the rules and kept that all to himself.

As the team of white coats broke down the projector and Edison shook every hand in the lobby, Maddy was being eyed by the manager. Chase knew his boss lurked somewhere in the building so he was quick to move toward her. He saw her. She saw him. And Chase saw the whole thing going down. He stepped in front of the manager, causing him to bump into Chase, knocking him to the floor.

"Oh, I'm sorry, sir. Please forgive me."

The distraction gave Maddy a split second to duck into the crowd and disappear from sight.

"Clumsy little boy."

"Yes, I am. My parents are always saying that."

Ever snooty, he responded to Chase, "They're right."

"Sir, you seem so smart, may I ask you a question?

"Certainly, young man. What is it?"

"What's the tallest building in New York?"

The manager eyed Chase. He thought it might be some sort of trick or joke. Chase responded, "Well?"

"Like tall buildings, do you?"

"I do."

"Indeed. They move me too."

That was a strange way to describe a building, Chase thought.

"So which is the tallest?"

"That would be the Manhattan Life Insurance Building."

"Never heard of it."

"Never?"

"Is it famous?"

"It's the tallest — "

Chase interrupted " — Where is it?!"

"Down at No. 1 Wall Street. They just built it two years ago. 348 feet into the heavens."

Edison's team had begun the trip back home as they loaded onto the ferry, when Chase pulled Maddy aside. "Maddy, this is where I leave."

"WHAT?!"

"I gotta go, but I wanted to thank you for..."

"For what?"

"For being my friend."

"I don't understand. Where are you going?"

Chase pointed behind him. There stood the Manhattan Life Building.

"Why?"

"Cause it's the tallest."

She looked at the top of it. The building was impressive. When she looked down, Chase had already taken off. He was half a block away and running. Unknown to him, she took off after him.

"CHASE! WAIT!"

Maddy finally caught up and found Chase trying to jimmy the lock on the main door.

"What are you doing?"

"Go back to the ferry." Chase protested.

"What are you doing?"

"I have to get inside."

"Why?"

Chase had no good answer to offer so he refocused on the task of getting inside. Reaching into his backpack, he pulled out the buck knife and rapidly popped the lock. He slid inside, quickly followed by Maddy.

"You're not trying to steal something, are you?"

"No."

"Then what are you up to?"

"I need to find a sun."

"A sun?"

"Yes. Over a doorway or a window or some sort of gateway."

"Ok...and you won't tell me why?"

"I can't."

Maddy was confused but helped out her friend.

The building was the tallest in New York City so it was also big. Especially the first floor. And the second. And the third. This building had eighteen floors...this could take awhile.

And it did. Chase and Maddy searched the entire building, floor after floor until they stood on the rooftop. The only place they hadn't checked was the top spire that went another twenty feet in the air.

"Think it's up there?"

She said they hadn't found it yet, so maybe.

Minutes after climbing inside the spire, a small doorway led to an outside catwalk that circled the very top of the building. Chase found the sun symbol on top of the door. He knew this was the portal but somehow he had to walk through without Maddy seeing.

"What if you meet me downstairs?"

"Why?"

"I just need a few minutes alone."

"Why?"

"I just do. Please. I'll be down there shortly."

Maddy took a long time to decide. Chase's eyes pleaded with her to give him a minute. She finally relented, taking a few steps back toward the stairs.

Over her shoulder she heard, "Thanks...for everything."

Maddy had taken three steps out when she stopped. Chase's words: "for everything" didn't sound right. *Was he upset about his house? Was he mad at Edison for some reason and running away with his plans? Was he just crazy and committing suicide by jumping?* Whatever it was, she didn't like the feeling in her heart.

She turned to see Chase moving forward toward the little door. She leapt toward him and managed to grab hold of the backpack. He kept moving forward and so did she. Then it felt like they were falling. And falling. But it was dark and maybe, she just might have closed her eyes in fear that they were dropping off the Manhattan Life building and hurdling toward the street. But they weren't. And when she did open her eyes, she saw a very angry Chase glaring at her.

Chapter 10

"Why are you here with me?!"

That was a good question. Actually a great one. But Maddy had a great question for Chase as well. "Where is here?"

Chase looked around for the answer. "That doesn't matter as much as you being here!"

"Which is…?"

"I DON'T KNOW!"

"This doesn't look like New York City."

Maddy was right. Chase knew that. Moments ago, they were standing on top of the tallest building in Manhattan, now…a big river in front of them and a medieval castle behind them. They were in a city…sort of, but from what they could make out, a much older one than New York.

The fog was thick, really thick. Seeing any sort of distance would be more than difficult. Maddy continued, "Doesn't look like New York City at all."

Chase shook his head in agreement.

"Did I hit my head?"

Chase looked to his friend. He knew he had to come clean. About everything. "Maddy…sit down."

"Why?"

"I've got something to tell you. And when I'm done it might _feel_ like you hit your head."

Five minutes later, Maddy sprang to her feet, "WHAT!" She was off and running down a path along the riverbank. Chase scrambled to catch up to her. "WAIT!"

She stopped.

"You don't know where we are. Somebody could be waiting to kill us or capture us or worse!"

"What's worse than either of those?"

Chase didn't have that answer. He just wasn't good at being dramatic. At least not at a moment's notice. Then something came to him. "We could be back in time from 1896."

"That sounds amazing."

"It might. But Blacks may not be free."

Maddy's face went long. For all "the explorer" that burned inside her, she hadn't thought of that reality. It was now sinking in.

"But if anyone asks, we'll just say you're my slave."

Maddy really fired up at that suggestion. "I AM NOT YOUR PROPERTY!"

"I DIDN'T SAY YOU WERE!"

"YOU JUST DID!"

"I--!" Chase caught himself. "I didn't mean it like that—"

"But you just said—"

"—you know, I'm the guy who goes to school with black people. I live next door to them. _I_ let them in my house!"

"Them?!"

Chase was red. "You. Them. Blacks! Whites! Whatever! I was only saying that to keep you out of trouble until we find the portal and get you back home."

Maddy calmed. As did Chase. They were silent.

"You know how to get me home?"

"I think so."

"Really?"

"Yeah. I think so."

"So why aren't you home then…?"

Chase paused. "Because I'm trying to find my grandfather."

Again they stood silent until Chase started sweating, like the sun was beating down on his forehead. But it wasn't. They were surrounded by fog. "Let's go try and find out where we are…and how to get out of here."

As they ventured away from the riverbank, the fog grew thicker and thicker. But that wasn't the only problem they encountered. The fog, they could deal with, the smell was a different story. The air smelt like a stinking gas. Rotten eggs. Old garbage. Grandpa Wally's manure pile behind the horse barn. It entered their noses and sat there. They couldn't shake it. It was there to stay.

It was about that time Maddy realized what they were walking through wasn't fog. It was smog. Or more clearly, the gas that they smelt. It was so thick and strong, it was almost solid, just hanging in the air.

"I'll take New York any day," she offered.

Chase took it farther. He'd even settle for another round of cleaning the horse barn rather than this place.

Some of their discoveries weren't all bad though. The street signs and businesses were written in English. At least, they knew the language.

"I kinda think this is London..."

Maddy asked him why he thought that.

"Just a guess. I'm pretty sure we are somewhere in England....by the signs."

"This place is creepy."

Chase had to agree. The buildings seemed to hover over top of them, like drooping trees in a dense forest. One false move and they'd be scooped up and never heard from again. Without knowing it, they had nudged closer and closer to each other as they walked the barren streets. At one point, Chase stopped dead in his tracks.

Maddy quickly asked, "What?"

"I thought I heard something."

"What?" she whispered.

"I don't know. Footsteps."

Maddy whipped her head around. There was nobody there. Then again, she could only see five or six feet in front of her or behind her.

"C'mon…"

They took another ten steps before Chase stopped again, listening and looking all around…and freaking Maddy out.

"Will you stop that?!"

"I <u>thought</u> I heard something."

"Then let's get out of here."

"Where's here? And where are we going?"

Maddy righted him, "To see if we can find your grandfather. To find the tallest building. To get home!"

Chase snapped to attention. He was acting paranoid, still looking around. He was listening to the streets as much as he was listening to her. It was eerily quiet. Then, they both thought they heard footsteps getting louder and louder.

"Chase. Chase!" He focused, looking into her eyes. "Chase, I don't feel safe here. Can we get going?"

He nodded. They began walking. Faster and faster…into the fog, still no idea where they were headed. Just away from where they were!

Disoriented, the kids turned down the street to again come upon the Tower of London. They had made a complete circle and ended back to their starting point. But something was different as they arrived at this spot again. The gas lamps around the tower had now been turned off as streaks of light begin to appear in the eastern sky. A few more steps and they now understood why. The lamp man shuffled up the walk, turning off the gas line.

"Excuse me, sir?"

When the hunchbacked man turned around, he frightened the kids. His eyes were crossed. His teeth were crooked and his scowl was evil. A big forehead with a bigger eyebrow. All the way across his head. From the start of one eye to the end of the other.

"HUH?!" He growled.

They leapt back. This guy was hideous.

"Where...are...we?"

"Whitechapel."

"Which is where?"

"In the East End."

"Of...?"

"London. The East End of London." He looked them over in disdain. "You are in Whitechapel. Are you morons?"

Chase sheepishly smiled. Maddy did not, "Guess we are. And as long as we are, what year is it?"

The lamp man scrunched his one eyebrow up and leaned closer to her face. Maddy didn't blink. "1888. Now be gone!"

The kids gladly complied and headed off in the opposite direction.

London was waking up this morning. More and more people were exiting their homes and entering the day. The fog lifted as the sun rose. It was actually visible as the cloudy sky continued to lighten. And with the light, came more and more visibility. They could begin to see greater distances. Close by, they could see the rickety homes along the streets. Bricks had fallen off, the buildings were crumbling. This was not the best that London had to offer its newest visitors. The more they walked, the more it looked like a ghetto.

Blocks away, they could see a mass of people gathered. Some were marching and some were shouting and some were doing both. A block closer and they could see all the participants were women. Curiosity got the best of the kids, and they continued to approach, hearing one constant chant: "White Slavery in London!"

Maddy learned from one of the strikers that this was the London Match Girls Strike. That if things kept up, all these poor women would be homeless within a month. The strike was caused by the poor working conditions in the match factory.

"They make us work fourteen-hour work days! They don't pay us and the conditions are unhealthy!"

"We're 1,400 strong and we're together!"

Another woman added, "When we don't show up for work, they fine us!"

The first woman piled on, "They're the ones giving us Phossy Jaw!"

Maddy asked, "Phossy Jaw?"

"Phossy Jaw makes your jaw glow. Green and white."

"It comes from vapors. Phosphorus. The jaw gets puffy. It becomes pus. Ya grow big sores. If you don't have the jaw removed, it'll kill ya."

About the moment she said 'kill,' a stampede came up from behind. It was the police. And they were about 500 strong. Outnumbered by the strikers but much bigger in size, stature and clubs. They were quite a force. Furious and ready to fight, the police moved the masses. Mob mentality took root in these situations and anger and fear replaced calm and cool.

Chase and Maddy were caught in the middle. Elbows and fists flew below, sticks and stones above. A relatively calm crowd ignited in a few short moments and chaos reigned. With guts and guile, Chase and Maddy wiggled their way free of the police and the mob and away from the skirmish.

"Let's get going!"

"No doubt."

The side alley provided the quickest escape route and they ducked down it. A couple hundred feet away, Chase stopped again, looking back. The alley curved so Chase couldn't tell what was behind them.

"What is it?"

"I thought I heard someone following me."

"Now your brain is playing tricks on you."

As they turned to walk on, a horse carriage whizzed toward them, screeching to a halt right in front of them. They were almost run over. Without speaking, Chase and Maddy both glanced at each other with shock. Flashbacks of the runaway wagon led by crazed horses through the streets of New York City, crossed both their minds. Those looks were not lost on the inhabitants of the carriage. A lady poked her head out of the back.

"Are you lost?"

Whether it was the shock from almost being run over or the American accent, the kids were too confused to answer.

"You kids look lost. Where are you going?"

"Home."

"Home? Where are you from?"

They kids were quiet again.

"Excuse me children, where do you live?"

"East Orange," Maddy answered.

"Is that nearby?"

She shook her head.

"And what about you, young man?"

"New York."

"New York? In America?"

Chase nodded yes.

The lady's face opened into a huge smile. "That's where we reside. Oh Ellen, do you hear that? This young man is from the States!"

Inside, Chase and Maddy sat across from the two ladies as the carriage rumbled through the cobblestone streets of the East End. They introduced themselves as Jane Addams and Ellen Starr. They were both 27 years old and from Chicago, Illinois.

"So where are your parents?"

The kids said nothing.

"Are you orphans?"

Again, nothing from Chase and Maddy.

"Do you have a place to stay?"

The hesitation from the kids gave Jane the split second to interject. "Have no worries. We have the perfect place. We're going there now."

The carriage pulled to a halt. The sign read: "Toynbee Hall." The house stood proud and inviting. A gothic style structure with vines creeping up the stone walls and chimneys poking out from the steep roof made of black shingle tiles. As they crossed the walk, Jane mentioned that Toynbee was the first settlement house in Europe. She said the kids can spend a night there free of charge.

All four entered the foyer to see the poor and homeless, a lot like the people they just saw at the match factory strike. Street kids, or urchins as they were called, ran and played in ratty clothes, carrying a layer of dirt on their skin.

"People who come here are malnourished. They receive a meal at night and one in the morning. There is a warm place for them to rest out of the rain."

"And the stinky gas," added Chase.

"Ahh…yes." Jane replied. "But the true brilliance is helping these people to make a difference in their lives first, then allow them to help others."

Chase and Maddy shuffled into the main room to see a plaque above the fireplace. It read: 'To learn as much as to teach; to receive as much as to give.'

Ever the motherly type, Jane guided the kids toward the kitchen. Two tired kids finally got some sleep after a solid meal of potatoes and meat stew. Their heads hit the pillow and they were out.

As evening fell, the hall began to grow in numbers. People came for meals but some stayed for the social time and some listened as various women began teaching classes. Toynbee offered classes for the adults and activities for the children.

Once awake, Chase rose and wandered through the various rooms looking for Maddy. He found her entertaining the kids. She was drawing goofy little pictures and making the kids laugh. Not wanting to miss the fun, Chase dug into his backpack. He pulled out a handful of bubble gum and a couple of rolls of lifesavers. The kids devoured them.

"Chase!"

Jane called him from the other side of the room. "The boy's club is meeting upstairs. Why don't you join them?"

"Why? Can't I stay here?"

"Chase, things don't work that way at Toynbee."

"I thought you were from Chicago?"

"I am."

"So why does it seem like you run the place?"

She smiled. "The boys are meeting upstairs. I believe they are playing billiards this evening after their lessons."

Chase entered to see the lesson had long concluded. The boys had already started the games.

"Billiards, young chap. Care to play?" One of the older teenagers approached Chase.

Chase had to ask, "Billiards is pool?"

"That's a slightly different game that they play in the States. But as I can hear by your accent, you must call that home."

Chase nodded.

"Can I ask you a question?"

The older boy agreed.

"What's the tallest building in London?"

"Well, that would have to be Big Ben."

"Big Ben?"

"The clock tower at Parliament."

Another teenager stuck his nose in to correct, "Technically, the Victoria Tower is several meters higher."

"Is the Victoria Tower close by?" Chase wondered.

"They are right next to each other. Just down the Thames."

"How long would it take to get there?"

"About thirty minutes by foot."

Chase looked at the clock. He calculated as the teenager asked another question. "You're not thinking of going tonight, are you?"

Chase wondered why not.

The nosy teenager dropped a copy of the London Times in front of him. The headline read: *Murder in Whitechapel!*

"If you go, beware of the Ripper."

Chapter 11

"The Ripper?!"

Chase stood stunned. He'd heard of the man from his friends but not much more. And it sounded like a story right our of a late night horror film except this was really happening. And this man...or creature walked the same dark streets that he and Maddy had walked this morning.

The older teenager continued. "Jack the Ripper. He's killed three and hasn't been caught yet."

Chase read, "The article says he only murders women."

"So far." The older boy then added in an ominous tone, "But do you want to risk it?"

Chase thought about it.

Downstairs, Maddy and a few girls had taken Chase's colored pencils to enhance their drawings. Jane roamed the various rooms, watching the children amidst various projects. She stopped to watch Maddy working with the younger girls. She was impressed.

After a few minutes of watching, Jane decided to join her, "What are you ladies drawing?"

"Flowers," answered the two small girls in unison.

"This was the place I used to work at back home." *It was Edison's laboratory.*

Jane became concerned and her voice changed to a motherly tone. "You're an impressive young lady. Intelligent and compassionate. How old are you?"

"Thirteen."

"And how are you so far from home?"

"I can't say."

"Are you an orphan?"

Maddy was silent.

"Is your mother here?"

"No. Not in London."

"Did you run away from home?"

Maddy wanted to change the subject. "Can we talk about something else?"

Jane stopped. "Of course. What would you like to talk about?"

Ever precocious and slightly defensive, Maddy definitely wanted the subject changed. "You. Why are you over here?"

"I came here for surgery."

Maddy softened, "Really? What's wrong?"

"I have a bad back. I came here to have spinal surgery."

"Did it work?"

"I hope so. It's still pretty painful."

"So why don't you go home?"

"I will. But I couldn't leave London without visiting Toynbee."

"You stayed in London for this place?"

"The good we secure for ourselves is precarious and uncertain until it is secured for all of us and incorporated into our common life."

Maddy was smart. Real smart. But Jane's words made her scrunch her face. "Meaning...?"

"I've been thinking about starting one in America."

"Where?"

"Chicago."

"You should make yours better than this."

Jane thought for a moment. "How?"

"Make sure girls are treated the same. This place only has a boy's club. What about the girls?"

Jane agreed. "You should join me."

Maddy looked confusingly at this woman.

Jane continued, "Maddy, what do you want to be when you grow up?"

"A famous inventor."

"Why?"

"Ahh...because I can make things that help people."

"What kind of things?"

"I don't know yet. But things that will make people's life easier."

"You want to help the poor and the underprivileged?"

"Yes."

"People who aren't strong enough to help themselves."

Maddy nodded yes.

"And immigrants?"

"I guess."

"And people who face racism and inequality?"

"Of course."

"Come with me. To Chicago. Back to America. Help me."

"Help you what?"

"Start it. Start this. A Toynbee Hall. Or one like it. But one that offers the same things for women and girls as it does for men and boys."

"Really?" Jane's offer tempted Maddy. She had never been respected for her thoughts and ideas by a grown-up like she was experiencing at this moment. And there was something about Jane that seemed completely genuine and real.

"Yes. Help me, Madeline."

"I don't know."

"You'll change people's lives."

"I will?"

"To quote you, of course."

"I don't know…"

"You'll have a place to stay. We'll make sure you get a good education. High school and college. And you can make the world a better place for little girls."

For as confident as Maddy always appeared, she was still an insecure young lady like every other girl or boy. Thus, she answered with more doubt than ever, "Me?"

"You are such an excellent example of what a young woman should be. I want every little girl to see that."

Maddy was quiet. Thinking. Pondering. This could be the fastest way back to America and close to the time in which she was born. She'd get to help people. She'd go to college. She'd have all of her dreams fulfilled. Hmmm…

"And playgrounds."

Jane and Maddy looked up to find Chase had joined them.

"Kids really love playgrounds. The bigger, the better. Jungle gyms. Swing sets. Ropes and ladders."

Chase just sounded like he was speaking Greek. And because of that, Jane and Maddy said nothing.

Behind Chase, appeared the carriage coachmen in the front hall. Seeing their coachman in the front hall, Jane rose, bad back and all, "Well, it's late. I must find Ellen and get back to our boarding house."

Once they were alone, Maddy again felt Chase hovering over her shoulder and checking out her artwork. She was quickly irritated.

Snottily she asked, "How was your little boys club?"

"It was alright."

"What did you "special" boys do?"

Chase shrugged off her sarcasm. "Nothing special."

"I bet."

Then Chase remembered his earlier conversation, leaned in and whispered to Maddy. "You ever heard of Jack the Ripper?"

Maddy shook her head no. Chase relayed the story of The Ripper and all the stories from the newspaper. He told about the fear that was gripping London. How women wouldn't go out alone. How three women had been killed and no one had been caught. And how the police weren't close to identifying any suspects.

As Chase spoke, Maddy inched to the edge of her seat. "Do you think he was following us early this morning?"

Chase hadn't thought of that. Now, _he_ was a little freaked.

Twenty minutes later, the kids were very happy that they were safe and sound in Toynbee Hall. The two artists were hard at work on their drawings. Maddy was still working on the picture of Edison's laboratory and Chase had started a drawing of the artistry inside the Parthenon. Deep in focus, their concentration was only broken when the front door burst open and quickly slammed shut. The coachman had returned, but was in a flurry of activity.

Maddy and Chase overheard the coachman talk to another of the Toynbee Hall attendants. They carriage had a faulty wheel and it broke down on Whitechapel Road. He had come back for a tool and told the ladies to stay put.

The attendant then asked in horror, "So you just left them there!"

The coachman tried to explain, "I had to. It was either that or we would sit there all night. That Addams woman can't walk long distances."

"But the Ripper's out there!" cried the attendant.

"WE GOTTA GO!" Maddy shouted to Chase.

He agreed immediately and shoved all of their things into the backpack. Before the coachman and attendant could turn around, the front door slammed open.

Chase and Maddy didn't just run down the streets, they broke world's records. Not much time was lost between when the coachman left and the kids arrived but it didn't matter.

The broken down carriage sat on the side of the road. Dimly lit, the kids peek around the corner of the building, barely making its outline. Slowly, their eyes peered to the left and then the right. They were looking for motion. Something. Anything. They were unsuccessful. The streets were too dark because the gas lamps weren't working. They had been blown out by the wind.

Maybe the ladies protested and decided they would walk the rest of the way back to their boarding house or maybe they didn't. Maybe they didn't make it back to their boarding house at all. Maybe a nice stranger in another carriage picked them up on his way home. Or maybe someone with bad intentions passed by…like The Ripper!

The kids could have created a thousand different scenarios but one thing was for sure: Jane and Ellen were gone!

"We've got to find them!"

Then, they saw the real reason the streets were so dark. A figure, dark and tall, wrapped in a topcoat that hung down like a cape past his knees moved swiftly down the street. The only sound he made was his hard soles hitting the cobblestones that made up the street. That was until: WHACK!

The dark figure held a cane in his hand, but he wasn't using it for walking. He had just crushed the glass of the gas lamp, shattering it into a million pieces. The light no longer lit the section of the street in front of the carriage. No light in front, no light in back. The perfect dark spot…for a serial killer.

The kids couldn't see what he was doing next but they heard something. He rustled through the carriage only to slam the door shut. Chase grabbed Maddy's arm. The kids looked at each other as best they could.

Chase whispered, "He doesn't have them yet."

Maddy whispered back, "We have to follow him and make sure he never does."

Chase protested, "We don't even know if that's Jack the Ripper."

Maddy countered. "He certainly looks like he could be."

"And you want to mess with him?"

"No. But I don't want Jane and Ellen to be killed."

"What about us?"

"We can just jump through the portal."

Chase thought about the escape.

"You know where it is, don't you?"

"I think so."

"Good, then let's get going. We gotta save my friends."

Then Chase was snarky...and a little jealous, "They're your friends now?"

"No...yes. They are my friends. And I might just go home with them."

"WHAT?! You're going to leave me? For them?"

"What do you care! You don't own me. And plus, you were mad when I came here with you anyway."

"Well...yeah, but now I thought we were..." Then something hit Chase, "we're not supposed to change anything. 'Leave only footprints.' I think you're more than footprints. Besides, you would be going back in time. You'd make yourself older."

Maddy hadn't thought of that. "I guess I would."

Chase took it one step farther. "I wonder if there's a baby Maddy in New Jersey right now?"

That stopped her in her tracks. She kept thinking about that conundrum. That was until they heard another crash farther down the street.

"C'mon, Chase. We have to help them."

"Fine." He grumbled.

The kids ran as fast as they could. And as quietly as they could. They looked funny running without letting their heels hit the ground loudly, but it was very effective. They made up a lot of ground, and trailed the figure by only a hundred feet. When he thought he heard someone behind them, they were also agile enough to duck into a doorway. Still panting heavily, the kids pressed themselves against the door. They didn't want to be seen or heard. After a few moments of catching their breath and keeping out of view, they crept out and followed the dark figure.

Two or three more repeated times hiding and the kids were far from Toynbee Hall, far from the carriage and far from knowing where they were. They were, however, close to being scared out of their socks. And each time they returned to following the figure, they were getting closer and closer to him. And he was getting more and more suspicious that someone was tailing him because he'd stop and turn, scanning the blackness. Luckily for Chase and Maddy, the same broken lamps that kept the streets dark for him, kept them unseen as well.

As the dark figure approached an intersection, the cross light shone on two women: Jane and Ellen. Moving slowly, Jane's back looked to be causing her pain and slowing their progress.

The figure sped up. He was focused and locked on the ladies.

Whispering as loud as she could, Maddy grabbed Chase's arm, "We gotta stop him."

"Ok. How?"

"Yell!"

Chase thought she was crazy. "What?!"

"Distract him. So they can go free and he chases us."

Chase stared at her. Now he knew. This girl _WAS_ crazy.

"He can't catch us!"

Chase knew she was right. "Turn around." Maddy had been carrying the backpack and now Chase was rifling through it.

"What are you looking for?"

"This!" She turned around to see Chase with the homemade slingshot.

"Can you hit him?"

"I think so."

Chase reached down and grabbed a loose stone off the street. He loaded, aimed and fired.

CRASH!

He didn't hit the dark figure. He didn't come close but he did break a window of the butcher shop that was between the figure and the ladies. It caused a distraction. It stopped both of them in their tracks. They both turned to look behind them. They saw nothing of the kids. But they did see the dark figure. And the dark figure knew he had been spotted.

The ladies were chilled to the bone with the creepiness the dark figure emitted and began to move quickly. The figure, sensed he had 'been made.' He had to act quickly. He started after Jane and Ellen. And he would have gotten to them in no time if another stone hadn't pelted him in the leg.

"Owwwww!" He looked back in time to catch another stone right in his nose.

Double "Owwwwww." That one seemed to hurt even more. When the third stone hit his ear, he had forgotten about the ladies completely. He was under attack!

Chase and Maddy had a process. She would find the stones and Chase would shoot them. That way, he'd never lose sight of the target in the darkness.

That wasn't going to be hard anymore because the target was heading toward them.

Chase whispered, "One more and then we run." He

loaded and shot but the moving target was hard to judge. The stone whizzed right by his right arm.

"Another! Give me another!"

She bent down to find more ammo when the dark figure ran toward them. It was still dark where they stood, so finding a stone was proving difficult.

As Chase kept talking though, he was providing audio clues on their location and the figure was dialed into his whispers. Ten more steps and the figure would be on top of them. Chase needed a stone and he needed it fast! He didn't get it…but what he got was a little luck.

"Maddy!"

Chase was the only one talking and thus he was the focus of the figure. Maddy, however, was down on her knees looking for another stone...quietly. She didn't see how close the figure was but more importantly, the figure didn't see her.

As he lunged for Chase, his foot hit her on a dead run and he went flying. Chase sidestepped him and grabbed Maddy. They took off running as his face planted against the cobblestone street. He slowly picked himself off the ground. His face was bruised and bloody. And he was mad! He tore off after them.

Chase and Maddy hit the intersection in no time. Chase had taken a hard left when he noticed Maddy was not right next to him. She had stopped and was staring down the other way.

"Maddy! Come on!" She did, but not before making sure Jane and Ellen were nowhere to be seen. The pause allowed the figure to rise to his feet and start chasing. Chase's voice again provided their location.

The kids ran. And ran fast. They had no idea where they were or where they were going. They were just going there fast. Taking rights and lefts, anything to lose the dark figure that was in pursuit. As they ran, Chase and Maddy were mainly looking backward, over their shoulders. The figure kept an even pace, never on top of them, but never more than twenty or thirty feet back. And because they were distracted, they hadn't noticed that one of the lefts they took led directly to a dead end. It was an alley, cramped and narrow, and blocked at the end by a brick wall.

Hoping the figure hadn't seen this mistake was a wish that was not going to come true. He knew these streets. And he had seen their mistake. Letting them wait, he wiped his lip of blood, adjusted his gloves and began to stroll down the alley. Payback was on the agenda.

Chase stood in the only stream of light that had made its way down from above. Maddy had to be in the shadows but he knew she was close by. As the figure came closer, he seemed to grow. Not just getting bigger, the closer he got, no, he seemed to come off the ground and hover over Chase. Chase had to keep looking up at this guy. His neck continued to crane higher and higher just to maintain eye contact. It looked like Chase's adventure through time was about to end. Unless…Chase and Maddy had a plan.

They did, but they had devised it quickly so there's no saying it was any good. He hid the slingshot behind his back. It was loaded. He was ready. A quick aim and fire. He just had to hit him. Right between the eyes. If he did, perfect. If he didn't…

He didn't. He missed. The stone whizzed right by the dark figure's face once again. But this time, he didn't trip over Maddy. She wasn't kneeling on the ground. She wasn't close enough to trip him.

However, she was close enough to throw the contents of a chimney sweep's ash can at the dark figure. Right in the face!

The dark figure got a whole lot darker. A black cloud of ash covered the coat, hat and face of the ominous man. The soot was in his mouth, nose and most importantly, his eyes. He was stunned and wounded. If he was "Jack the Ripper," he would not be bothering anyone else this evening. He probably wouldn't be out and about for quite some time. He stumbled backwards in pain. Chase picked up another stone and took a point blank shot. He was on target this time. Right between the eyes! That stone was the straw that broke the camel's back. The dark figure toppled over and lost his footing. The kids had successfully dropped him on his backside to writhe in pain.

They rushed from the alley way, and took the turn they should have in the first place. The street opened up to the river Thames and down the half bend, Big Ben and Parliament stood lit up for all to see. Majestic, Victoria Tower stood at the south end of the Parliament Building. They raced past the sign that read Palace of Westminster, past the clock tower that they called "Big Ben" and straight down Abingdon Street. Chase and Maddy grabbed hands as they ran through the arched doorway. This time they didn't need to look for the portal. By running through that arch, they had found it.

Boom! They were in the darkness again. Just like on Whitechapel Road. When they stopped, they stood on the hill of a rolling countryside. Greens and browns. Fields and small forests. Groves of trees and shrubs with plenty of grassy meadows. Behind them stood a small farmhouse and barn.

"Not London."

"Or New York."

"Not even close."

"Nope. This is the middle of nowhere."

"Middle of nowhere, indeed."

Chapter 12

"Middle of nowhere, indeed."

"Well, let's get going and find out just how far away we are from the middle of nowhere."

"Yeah…"

As they walked up one hill and down another, the countryside seemed to roll on forever. Four hills later, Chase remembered his compass and pulled it out. He had no map to consult but at least he could determine their direction. They were walking west.

"That makes sense because the sun is slowly setting ahead us." Chase looked up at the sun, then to Maddy and back to the sun. *Man, she was a smart one. Nothing gets by her. (And he would not be admitting that to her either!)*

As these thoughts were popping into and out of Chase's head, he wasn't playing attention to his surroundings. "Chase, look at those birds."

Maddy was pointing up to the sky. Just to the left of the sun, several large birds were soaring over the grassy hill. They were large birds, swooping and diving. Not for food, like they were killing their prey. No, they looked like they were playing with which other.

"It's like they are dancing in the sky."

"Or wrestling." Chase added.

"The birds are playing tag!"

Both Maddy and Chase's eyes were focused on the birds when they took their next steps. Steps that included Maddy stepping on a stack of loose parchment papers lying inside a leather folder and knocking over a small inkwell, spilling the contents into the dirt.

That wasn't as upsetting to the scene as Chase. He stepped on the chest and stomach of the old man lying in the grass on his back. The old man gasped. Flinched. And pushed Chase off him. Chase went flying, his face planting itself in the ground, dirt spraying into his eyes, nose and mouth.

Everyone startled, they bounced up, turning to face each other. A moment of tension and eyeballing, until the old man opened up a huge smile, chuckling loudly.

Chase and Maddy unclenched and released. He seemed friendly. His face was happy and light. Long gray hair on his head. Shorter gray hair on his chin and cheeks. His eyes, deeply calm.

"Buon pomeriggio."

The kids stared. The words sounded pleasant and cheerful but they had no idea what he's saying.

"Hello...?"

"Halo?" The old man repeated.

"Hello."

"Germania?"

They didn't respond.

"Britannico?"

"Britain? English?"

The old man understood, "Inglese. Yes. Inglese. I speak a little."

"Can you help us?"

"Help?" The old man didn't quite understand. Chase went to his Latin class work: "help...food...assistance?"

Now the old man got it, "ahhh... assistenza." He began running down the hill. Maddy and Chase watched in wonder until he stopped long enough to wave at them to follow. "Si! Si!" Then he mentioned something about following or hurrying, but Chase couldn't quite make it out. His motions were enough.

When the three arrived at the wide dirt road, a sense of calm came over Chase and Maddy. The city limits of the old man's town sat a few hundred meters away. The town was impressive from afar. Not as big as Athens but the buildings rose higher. Three, four and five stories lined similar small streets and tight alleys.

The roofs shimmered in the setting sun. There were red clay and curved tiles on the sandy white plastered walls. The closer they got, the more foot traffic they encountered. Olive skinned and dark haired, the citizens of the town moved with purpose and passion. Their arrivals home were met with joy and embrace.

The old man saw the kids observing this, "la familia!"

Chase nodded, "Family."

"Yes."

"What town is this?" Chase's brain stretched, "nome?"

"Nome? La citta?"

"Si," Chase answered.

The old man spoke with the passion of the mayor, "Firenze!"

As they continued walking, the three passed the center of town and a large basilica and an equally tall bell tower.

The old man played tour guide. He pointed, "Santa Maria del Fiore Cathedral."

Chase pointed to the tower. "Nome?"

"Il campanile di Giotto."

Maddy nudged him for a translation. Chase complied, "Giotto's Bell Tower...I think."

Chase marveled at the height. And in his head, he got excited. He was thinking he had just found the site of the portal. He motioned to the old man as if to ask if they could go inside.

The old man smiled. "Si si." The door was locked but a quick jimmy by the old man and the door creaked open. As the kids pushed in, the old man placed his finger to his lips. This translation was universal and the kids remained quiet.

They climbed the steps, as Chase searched the jambs of the doors and windows. He was so blatant that Maddy asked him to stop what he was doing.

"Looking for a sun."

"But we just got here."

Chase was getting annoyed, "Just look for it."

Maddy rolled her eyes at Chase but complied with his instructions.

"This time travel is pretty fun if you ask me."

Chase muttered, "I didn't."

As they arrived at the top, the old man showed off his city. And the view was amazing. Full orange sky, the sun had disappeared under the horizon, but it still sprayed its light on the western sky. Those hills that were green all afternoon were now turning shades of purple and blue. The moon was rising in the southern sky. Maddy stood next to the old man taking in the view.

Chase, however, was at the northern windows. He thought he'd spotted the object of his search. It looked like half of an etching of the sun. The other half had deteriorated when the plaster crumbled off the wall. Chase called Maddy over to show her the discovery. She agreed with him...sort of. Chase was certain. When she asked so what, he began to explain that she was the new one. He'd done this before.

"How many more times?" She asked.

"Two."

"Only two?"

"Trust me."

The old man stood a few feet away trying to make out what was being said. These kids were arguing. Chase wanting to jump immediately, while Maddy telling him he was crazy. They were getting more and more animated when Maddy put her foot down. She was not jumping out of that window without a parachute!

"Parachute? Par-a-chute?"

They both looked at the old man.

Then answered, "Yes."

Maddy used her hands to show a parachute. One hand opened wide, facing down. The other hand resembling a small person. She pretended that it was thrown out of the window, mocking that it fell slowly to the Earth.

The old man's eyes popped. He began rifling through his papers. Papers full of sketches. First of people. Faces. Arms. Legs. Full bodies. Muscles in different movements and motions. Both kids, being artists, were sucked in immediately.

After the human forms, the drawings were more mechanical. Bridges and buildings. Machines like catapults and levers. Then birds. Lots and lots of birds. Wings and bird bodies. Wings with feathers and wings without. Lots and lots of wings. Then something that looked like a helicopter. A very weird looking one but a helicopter nonetheless. He was an amazing artist. His drawings were awesome.

Finally, the old man got to the parachute. He was excited. Both kids wondered why. They both said yes and thought nothing of it. But the old man didn't stop there. He ripped the bottom of his shirt and then another rip until he had made a small linen square. He looked around the top floor and found an empty wine bottle...well mostly empty. He pulled the cork and took a swig. His scrunched face showed it wasn't good, but it wasn't bad. He offered the bottle to the kids but they both quickly declined.

He took the cork and used it as the fake person. The leather string that held his folder together became the tie that attached the linen parachute to the cork. They all looked as he held it out the window and dropped it. It fell fast. Too fast.

The cloth wasn't big enough, Chase evaluated. He reached into his backpack and pulled out the small toy pewter clipper ship. They were going to try again. But with the weight of the toy ship, the parachute was going to have to be much bigger. The old man took off his shirt. He was offering the whole shirt.

Chase went back into his backpack and pulled out a few rubber bands. He assembled the second version of the parachute. The old man was paying attention. He was examining the rubber bands, completely fascinated by the little loops.

When Chase finished, the old man stood impressed. All three were smiling. Chase took the little flying ship and launched it out the window. All three jumped up to see the results of the experiment. And then they saw something else. The projectile was falling. Not too fast but not too slow. And it was heading right for a man who had been walking by but now had stopped.

He was a city police officer. And it hit him right on the top of the head. The Old Man must have known something because he pulled the kids back from the window so they wouldn't be seen.

The officer rubbed his head, studying the parachuting toy ship that had just hit him. Then he looked up and yelled, "Leonardo!"

The Old Man peeked out the window and smiled. The officer pointed at the ground. Leonardo knew his presence was being requested on the ground.

When they get down, the police officer scolded the Old Man.

"Leonardo, you know better than this. You know you are not allowed in the tower without the permission of Signore Machiavelli. That tower is Firenza property."

The old man hung his head. He attempted to explain something about an experiment, but the officer didn't want to hear it. In fact, he tired of Leonardo's excuse as the first words left his mouth. No, the officer was more focused on the two young people also in front of him.

He began to interrogate Leonardo in Italian. "Who's the boy?"

"He's a visitor."

"From where?"

"Far away."

The officer wanted more explanation than that.

"I don't know exactly but he speaks other languages."

The officer's glare fixed on Chase, his hand club patting the palm of his other hand. "Which ones?"

"Italiano. Inglese. And more."

"So he's a foreigner?"

"Or from an educated family."

This caught the officer's attention. "Oh yeah...which

one?"

"He hasn't said, but there's only one family rich enough for a boy to have a servant."

"So the Negro is with him?"

"Yes."

"Why does he need an Africana?"

Leonardo said nothing but his face implied what the officer was thinking. Leonardo whispered to the officer. "He must be a young Medici. Look how he's dressed and how he has a servant."

Chase was getting about every third or fourth word. Maddy wasn't getting any of them, but Chase wasn't going to translate.

The officer finally tired of the interrogation and told them to go home. He finished his diatribe by saying something about a new curfew from Signore Machiavelli.

Leonardo perked up at the suggestion. He thanked the officer and quickly guided the kids down the cobblestone alley. Only a few steps away from the officer, Chase stopped. And headed back to the policeman. He reached out his hand. He was asking for the small parachute. Slowly the officer began to understand and handed him the linen. Chase shook his head no. The officer had taken the small pewter clipper ship and shoved in his pocket. He showed Chase that he had nothing else in his hands.

"Mi Nave?"

The officer pretended to know nothing of Chase's words or request. Chase knew he was lying. They were at an impasse. About this time, Leonardo attempted to guide Chase away again but Chase wouldn't have any of it. He was holding his ground. So was the officer.

He mentioned to Leonardo that it was a gift from his Grandfather. "Mi Nonno." But Leonardo told him it must be lost, wanting him to get away from the tower quickly. He promised they would find it in the morning.

A couple of lefts and rights and they were standing on the other side of town.

"Signore?"

The old man stopped, looking back at Chase.

"Signore? Food?" He made the universal symbol of bringing his hand to his mouth and pretending to chew.

"Si. Si. Mia casa." The old man pointed ahead on the road out of town. He again started walking down the dirt trail before turning around. Pointing to himself, "Leonardo. Mio nome, Leonardo." He then pointed to Chase, "Signore Medici?"

Chase completely missed that earlier. When the Leonardo was talking to the officer. He had heard "Medici" but didn't understand the name or the significance.

Chase corrected Leonardo. "Me, Chase. She's Maddy."

Maddy quickly inserted, "Madeline."

Leonardo nodded. "Chasio e Madeline." He said the names with the flair and style of the Italian language. Chase smiled. Maddy blushed. Then Leonardo leaned into Chase's ear. "Chasio Medici." He put his finger to his lips and offered his promise, sssshhh."

Again confused, Chase turned to Maddy. "Why does he keep thinking my last name is Medici?"

Maddy only shrugged.

The group walked up a small hill that faced the larger city of Florence. As they came through a small grove of trees, a long stone house stood in front of them. Three small but connected structures comprised Leonardo's home and studio. The kids followed the old man inside, happy to be at a place they could rest.

Leonardo began lighting candles throughout the house. When the room was fully lit, Chase and Maddy thought they were in a museum. Or an earlier version of Edison's lab. Or maybe a toy store.

Half of the objects in the drawings of the old man's notebook were sitting in this room in various stages or construction and assembly. Little wood models of his sketches. Flying machines. Bird wings. Wood that had been carved. And wood waiting to be carved. It was a room of wonder or a mad man's laboratory or maybe both. Chase and Maddy and their mechanical minds began to roam the room. Their eyes jumped from one small creation to the next. Their fingers touching and playing and feeling the models.

Leonardo watched the kids and their exploration with a huge smile on his face. The joy their faces exuded only increased his own.

Chase had just set down the two-foot bird wing when his eyes caught something in the back corner of the room. He slowly walked toward it. His eyes showed confusion and recognition.

On a small easel, sat a half finished painting. He had seen it before. At least, he thought he had seen it before.

Chapter 13

"Are you painting this?"

Leonardo nodded.

"I've seen this before."

Leonardo was confused. "How? I haven't finished it."

"Yeah, but the guy who first painted this did."

Leonardo was more confused.

Chase added, "It's really famous."

About this time, Chase got an elbow in his side. "He _is_ the guy who painted it."

"Really?"

"I thought it was really old."

"_We_ _are_ _traveling_ _through_ _time_," Maddy added.

"Oh yeah."

"And you've been speaking Italian, haven't you?"

"Latin. I've been speaking Latin."

"Doesn't Italian come directly from Latin?" She knew it did, but she had learned that it worked easier if she let Chase think he had come up with it first.

"Yeah. Yeah, it does. Italian. French. And Spanish."

"I think we're in Italy. I think this is about to become the Mona Lisa. And I think we are standing in the house of Leonardo Da Vinci."

Maddy was right. And they knew it because when she said his name, he lit up like an airport runway. He gave her a big hug and invited them to sit. He made motion that he was going to go and get food. Before they could say anything, he had run into the other room.

When they were sure he wasn't near, Chase asked. "_THE_ Da Vinci?"

"I think so."

"And that's the original Mona Lisa?"

"I think."

"You know how much that is worth?"

"I don't. But right now, I'd guess nothing, since it's not finished."

"Well...yeah. But when he's done with it... You know a guy could make a lot of money by traveling through time."

"I guess. But then you would be changing history."

"Not if it's something small. Just a little thing."

"Doesn't everything change history? Even something small?"

"You sound like my grandpa."

"But his rule book says to take nothing but memories and leave nothing but foot prints."

Chase was disappointed, "I know."

"I like that rule. Your grandpa sounds like a pretty smart man."

Chase agreed, "He is."

Leonardo entered the main room with plates of food. When he set them down, the kids saw a feast before them.

"Antipasto!"

The plates were heaped with cured meats. Sliced prosciutto and salami. Italian meats that both kids devoured. But Leonardo served more than meat. He brought out olives, roasted garlic, pepperoncinis, mushrooms, artichoke hearts and several cheeses like provolone and mozzarella. The food hit the spot and all three didn't talk. They inhaled.

With the food no longer on the plates but in their bellies, they leaned back in their chairs and sighed.

Chase stared at the unfinished Mona Lisa. Leonardo waited on his words, which came quickly, "Aren't you supposed to be painting?"

"Si."

"When are you going to finish the painting?"

"Someday."

"Soon?"

"Maybe, maybe not. It's not a very pretty woman. Her beauty does not inspire me."

Maddy had a question, "Then why finish it?"

"I have been paid by Signore Giocondo."

"And he doesn't want it soon?"

"He'll get it when it is completed. And no sooner!"

Leonardo got a little angry at that question so they decided to change the subject.

Maddy wondered aloud, "What year is it?"

"1505."

Chase added, "Really. So we're in the middle of the Renaissance?" He had remembered a story of his grandfather and the great artists of the time. He remembered Leonardo. And Michelangelo. And Raphael. He also thought about asking about the painting.

"Renaissance?! You too?"

Chase didn't have an idea what he said that irritated Leonardo even more.

"People are speaking of this. The great Italian Renaissance. The Renaissance because the paintings are bolder and brighter. That the great masters are changing. I am sick of it. Sick of it all. I don't want to talk of painting. Painting bores me."

"Ok, Leonardo. No painting. No talk on painting."

"If this is some grand renaissance, it will be more than just paintings, you know? Times change when people look forward. Think forward. Dream forward. When they are not fearful of the future."

Leonardo had worked himself into a frenzy when Chase got up and went back to the models. He picked up the small glider like contraption. Leonardo's eyes darted to him and the model. He stopped his rant immediately. And his mood changed instantly.

"Do you like?"

Chase nodded.

"Would you like to help?"

"Help with what?"

"Tomorrow. We fly this tomorrow."

"OK."

"So you will help?" Leonardo asked.

Chase nodded again. They both looked at Maddy. She agreed as well.

The sun was barely peaking over the horizon when the three marched back into the city. This time they were carrying a very large piece of linen cloth and ropes.

After a night of rest and that big meal, they had more energy and the trip seemed to go twice as quick. In no time, they stood outside the doors of Giotto's Bell Tower once again. The streets of Florence had not yet come to life. The kids surmised this was Leonardo's plan. Sneak in, experiment and get out of the city before the town had awoken up from the night.

Leonardo's magic fingers quickly dispatched the lock once again. He waved at the kids to move inside but Chase wasn't paying attention. He was searching the ground for his toy ship. Cortes' clipper. It was nowhere to be found.

Deep down, Chase knew that though. Because for all the money in the world you couldn't tell Chase anything else but that the officer had it in his pocket. He just knew it. It took both of them to get Chase back on task. Maddy helped Leonardo corral Chase inside.

Once they were inside, the three climbed the tower steps in record time and stood at the same window as they had the night before. Chase was sure to point out the sun carving above the window. In the morning light, Maddy had to concede it did look a lot like the sun symbol on the cover of the codebook.

Leonardo was on the other side of the floor building his man-size parachute. When he finished, he pulled the ropes toward Chase and began to wrap them around his shoulder and chest.

Chase protested, "Why me?!"

"You're the perfect size."

"Why not you?"

Leonardo raised his voice. "I am an old man!"

"So! This is your experiment!"

"But you are a boy! This should be second nature."

"But I could get hurt!"

Leonardo pleaded his case with the help of his notebook. "Not by my calculations. I've done this to my own height and weight."

Chase had a good comeback, "Then why don't you do it?"

"You're smaller than me and you weigh less. This will be an easy drop." Leonardo then turned on his Italian charm. He smiled and cowered and a twinkle formed in his eye. "And I'm an old man."

Chase finally relented. He let Leonardo continue the parachute assembly. As Leonardo circled Chase and the parachute, checking the knots and the ropes. As he did, Chase called Maddy near.

"Jump into my arms right before I leap."

Maddy looked at Chase like he was nuts. "Are you kidding me?! That's a long way to the ground."

"We won't hit the ground."

"What?!"

"We're jumping through the portal. We'll be ending up in some other land…in some other time. We won't hit the ground because we're going to be landing somewhere in the world far away from here."

Maddy considered Chase's logic.

Leonardo yelled at him to climb up on the windowsill. He did as he was told, but his eyes remained on Maddy.

"You don't want to be left here, do you?"

Now, she really had something to think about.

"I guess becoming Leonardo Da Vinci's assistant wouldn't be so bad. I mean I could say I helped Da Vinci and Edison."

"To who?" Chase countered. "to who could you say that? Who here will know who Thomas Edison is?"

"Well, I could become the world's greatest inventor by using all of the things Edison created and people would know the name Madeline Jackson everywhere."

"Take only memories. Leave only footprints. Last night you told me you liked that."

Maddy hated her own words being used against her.

"Besides, you're too smart and too honest to take other people's work and claim it as your own. That's stealing."

Her face dropped farther. He was making good points. Maybe he was smarter than she gave him credit for. "But to learn from Da Vinci…"

"You can't."

Maddy's eyes squinted at his words.

"They don't like you here."

"Huh?"

"Last night, the officer. He asked who you were and Leonardo explained you were my servant."

She glared back at the old man. "He what?!"

"He said it so we could get out of there."

Maddy fumed as Chase tried to calm her.

"There was something shady about that cop. He stole my toy ship. He looked evil and I could tell he was racist. I don't think this time is a good time for you."

Maddy's arms were crossed. She was on fire.

"That's why I'm telling you, you need to leap into my arms when I jump through the portal."

Chase stood on the edge of the windowsill. In his hands, he held a wad of linen and rope. Leonardo instructed him on how to jump. And how to launch the parachute into the air. If Chase didn't, he would fall too quickly. He must get the linen very high into the air. Chase kept nodding but in his head he could only think: He seems so nice...a nice old man but he's got a little mad scientist to him.

Chase whispered this to Maddy once and added reference Leonardo would not understand: "Like those old Frankenstein stories."

Maddy got it instantly, "I've read Frankenstein." Chase hadn't. He'd watched late at night on cable television. "There's a book too?"

"Jump, Chasio! Jump!"

Chase took a deep breath and looked at Maddy. As he was about to leap, he turned to open his arms to

Maddy. He did. But she didn't leap into them. She couldn't. Leonardo, out of excitement, had given her a big hug. Chase stumbled as he tried to maintain his balance. He didn't want to fall through the window and leave her behind. He had no idea how he would get back to her even if he wanted to. And when he hesitated, he tried to reach back for her. When this happened, he dropped the parachute. He didn't have the parachute. He didn't have the girl. And a split second later, he didn't have his balance. So Chase did the only thing he could. He fell. And fell. And fell.

Chase didn't hit the ground. But he wasn't transported either. That window wasn't the portal. Chase came to a stop. And there he hung. One hundred feet below the window. Two hundred feet above the ground.

Leonardo and Maddy peered over the window ledge.

Maddy offered compassion, "Are you hurt?"

Leonardo offered fear, "Hurry back up. Before the police catch us."

"The police?!"

Chapter 14

"The Police?!

"Yes. We're not supposed to be up here. And if they caught us, we'd probably be locked up. Well, we would. You are a Medici. Either you're family would buy your freedom or they'd kill you."

"Kill me?!"

"Along with your servant."

"Servant?!"

"Machiavelli doesn't like the Medici family."

"I'm not a Medici!"

"Then he'd probably kill you right away for pretending to be one."

"I wasn't pretending!"

"He doesn't know that."

All this talking wasn't getting Chase off the side of the building any faster. But the noise and time delay was allowing the city to wake up and hear the commotion in the city square.

Leonardo and Maddy strained to pull Chase up but they were not quick and ultimately not successful. From his perch, Chase could see the entire plaza. And he could see a group of officers heading right toward the bell tower. He warned the two inside to run. At first, they ignored his pleas but when he told Leonardo that Maddy could not be captured, he agreed and they rushed down the steps and slipped out a back door of the tower.

Before the officers arrived, Leonardo shouted to Chase one piece of advice. "When you meet Machiavelli, remember one thing. He loves power. It's his weakness."

A group of city militia arrived moments later and cut Chase loose. But he didn't stay "loose" for long. They grabbed him and immediately took him to the city jail.

The damp jail sat in the basement of the city building. Luckily for Chase, they put him in his own cramped cell. Not that the guards didn't scare him to death by showing the adult cells with the tough criminals that were locked up in a lower dungeon.

Chase spent all day in the small closet-like cell waiting...and waiting...and waiting. His backpack hung outside the cell, but just out of his reach. No DS. No pencils. No chewing gum. And no adventure. Just waiting. Bored and wondering.

The more Chase sat, the more Chase thought. He had been in some tight situations, but for some reason he always thought he'd get out of it. But today, at this moment, the feeling was different. The more he sat and stared at the walls, the more uneasy he felt. And who was this Machiavelli guy that Leonardo had warned him about?

The sun was setting by the time the officer from the night before arrived at his cell. The officer yanked Chase out and roughed him up as he led him through the narrow stone hallways of the jail basements, pulling him by his right arm.

With each step, Chase's legs got heavier. With each turn, fear crept into his brain. *Where was this guy taking me? When was he going to be let go?* They finally stopped in front of a small room with one chair. The officer forced him into the chair. Then hovered near.

Chase sat nervously for a few moments, checking out the surroundings. When he tried to get up, the officer forced him to sit again. Chase didn't like this for two reasons. First, who was this guy to tell him what he could and couldn't do. He never wanted to be here from the beginning. And secondly, he thought this guy was a jerk and a liar.

"Where's my ship?"

The officer didn't understand English.

"Mi nave?"

The officer smirked. He reached into his pocket and showed Chase his little toy. Chase lunged for it, but was unsuccessful. The officer laughed a little louder and tucked it back into his pocket.

"Jerk!"

The officer hadn't heard that word before but tried to mimic Chase. "Jeeerrrrkkk...?"

"You're a jerk."

"Jerk?!" Both Chase and the officer whipped their heads to the door. Standing there was a tall, thin man with very dark eyes and a narrow face. The cheekbones protruded, almost pointed and sharp. He wore a red robe with gold designs running down the front. His thin, bony fingers were adorned with several small gold rings with one major gold and garnet ring on his right fourth finger. The man looked evil. He looked mean. And he looked like the power hungry man Leonardo described.

A chill went up Chase's spine. The man seemed to know that because at the same time the chill reached Chase's spine, the evil man smiled. His timing was perfect. Chase's legs now were as heavy as concrete and fear was bouncing all over his brain.

In Italian, the man announced his name. He held both his arms out with his palms up. He appeared like an evil angel and stated, "Mi nome Machiavelli. Governor Machiavelli of Firenze."

"What do you want?"

Machiavelli then asked the boy for his name. Chase finally understood and replied, "Chase."

He then pointed at Chase, "Chasio Medici."

"No. No. No Medici."

Machiavelli laughed like the devil and said something that showed Chase he didn't believe him. Chase's head dropped. Not only could he not understand half of what this crazy man said, but whatever Chase did say in Latin wasn't believed. This was beginning to feel like one of those murder interrogations seen in a police drama television show.

"Am I in trouble?"

"Trouble?" Chase was asked.

"Si. Trouble. You're treating me like a criminal!"

"Ahh...criminale. Si, Signore Medici." Machiavelli pointed at Chase, "Criminale."

"Why?"

Machiavelli didn't understand.

"How come?"

"Come? You are a Medici!" Machiavelli got louder and angrier as he spoke. He said that Florence didn't like the Medici family.

"They were evil rulers and they took from the people." He told Chase how the Medici had ruled Florence for sixty years and how the people expelled them eight years prior. And he explained how Machiavelli always stood by the people.

"But I am not a Medici." Machiavelli did not understand. Chase yelled, "NO MEDICI!"

Machiavelli stopped and stared at Chase. His evil smile returned and he said three words, "Buono da male."

Chase tried to translate. He got that 'buono' meant good. That was easy. Da sounded like a connector so he figured it meant 'and' or 'or' or 'from' or something like that. It was 'male' where he stumbled. He sounded it out. "Mal...e. Mal...e." Then his Latin and Greek homework kicked in. Mal was a prefix on words that meant bad or evil. This guy was saying good and bad or good or bad or good from bad. It was the last one he thought. Good from bad. Whatever Machiavelli had in mind, this was not going to be good.

"Medici e male."

Machiavelli leaned down, his nose inches from Chase's nose. He stared with those evil dark eyes. He wanted Chase's full attention. "Medici ricevere strappado."

"I receive the strap?"

"STRAPPADO! DORMANI!"

"The strap. Tomorrow? What is the strap?"

Chase shouldn't have asked the question. He shouldn't have asked because the officer was all too ready to give him an example of tomorrow's punishment.

From behind, the officer grabbed both of Chase's arms and wrapped some of the parachute ropes around Chase's wrists. The officer pulled Chase's arms behind his back and upward. From the wrists, the officer lifted Chase off the chair and off his feet, forcing his arms to bear the body's weight.

This would dislocate Chase's shoulders if the officer hadn't stopped. Chase could hardly breathe. The pain was intense…and just in those few moments!

Chase slumped back into the chair, trying to recover. The officer still hovered behind him. Machiavelli stood back, watching the boy suffer, proud of his type of torture. "Strappado." He turned and walked out.

Chase was thrown back into his small cell before the officer returned to Machiavelli's office. When he entered, he was informed that Chase should receive the strappado technique until his arms were broken and the shoulders were separated. After that, if he hadn't died, he would be hanged.

The officer was very excited to carry out the punishment, but reminded Machiavelli that even a Medici should not be put to death on a Sunday. Machiavelli was clearly annoyed by the fact that tomorrow was a Sunday. He had no problem torturing on Sundays, but relented and decided Monday morning would be fine. Not great, but fine. No torture on Sunday is what the people of Firenze had expected.

Night fell and the tiny cell seemed to close in around Chase. It was not made any better by the mocking of the guard sitting down near his cell. Chase was the object of ridicule.

Teasing made the man of security tired. The day had worn away and sleep filled the guard's eyes. He leaned back in his chair and tried to catch a few minutes of sleep. This nap was a huge mistake. Or not the nap so much as the preparation for the nap. The guard threw Chase's backpack on the ground.

As a restless Chase paced his small cell, he walked near the bars and saw that the backpack had moved. And tossed within arm's reach. He quickly grabbed it.

At least his last few hours would be better, he thought. Chase grabbed his pencils and sketchbook and began drawing. First, he drew a few bricks of the cell but that wasn't making anything better. He switched to recreating some of Leonardo's drawings of birds and wings. He sketched the bell tower and the Basilica next door before scribbling a note to Grandpa Wally and his Mom and Dad.

It was sort of a last will and testament and a goodbye letter. He started mad, mainly at his Grandpa. Then the letter turned sad for not being able to see them again and even sadder when he realized these were his last few hours. Chase was full of self-pity. And he was sick of drawing and writing. And needed a break.

It was time for his DS. At least he could play a little Mario before falling asleep on the cold hard stones that made up the floor. The game distracted him for a few moments. But considering the current situation, even the game couldn't hold his attention. His night was really waning. As the guard snoozed, he dug through his backpack, looking for anything that might grab his eye or take him away from his current plight. He dug and dug but couldn't find any fresh ideas.

The only place he hadn't looked was the cigar box but as far as he could remember, Grandpa did not give him anything but little trinkets.

Oh well, Chase thought. *Might as well look. You never know…*

Chase rummaged unsuccessfully. He didn't find any batteries…but he did find a key ring. With four keys on it. He stared at them. *There's no way…*

Chase tried each key. The third proved to be lucky. It turned easy and smooth. The key unlocked the cell. Grandpa Wally was Chase's favorite person in the history of the world!

He snuck out of the cell as the guard kept sleeping. He was out, but he wasn't close to being free or from getting caught. Making sure to keep his backpack still and silent, Chase tiptoed through the narrow halls. He peeked around each corner, careful to avoid the small puddles and candle light that lit the passageway. He hid in the shadows, jumping from dark corner to dark corner.

The stairs were his last hurdle to the first floor and his freedom. Step after step, quickly but quietly, Chase edged up the circular stone steps. At the top of the stairs, a large, locked wood door stood between him and freedom. Chase tried another one of the keys and again: success! He unlocked the door and slowly pulled the creaky wooden structure inward.

Chase ducked his head out the door but heard footsteps coming from the cobblestone street. He disappeared back inside waiting for the person to pass. The footsteps did go away. The person didn't. He or she had stopped in front of the door. A key went inside and relocked the door. After a bit of fiddling, the lock clicked and the door slowly opened.

The person entered having no clue who lurked in the shadow. Chase, behind the door, spotted the man walking in. It was the officer. Instead of cowering, Chase acted without thinking. With all his strength, Chase shoved the door with his shoulder, trapping the officer between the wall and the heavy wooden door, knocking him out.

Chase began his escape with two running steps when something shiny caught his eyes. It was the small clipper ship. It had fallen out of the officer's pocket. Chase smiled before grabbing it and escaping Florence at a sprinter's pace.

Chase had to stop a few feet down the path to catch his breath as he snuck up to Leonardo's house. He didn't want the heavy breathing to wake the old man. He just needed to sneak in, get Maddy and get gone! FAST!

Chase reached the door and slowly unhooked the

lever. Slowly, his left hand gently pushed the heavy door open. A few inches cracked and Chase stopped. He waited and listened. The only sound was a rhythmic snore. *That had to be Leonardo.*

He opened the door a little wider, allowing the moonlight to shine inside but the house was still very dark. Like a cat burglar, Chase made his way to the small floor mat where Maddy was sleeping. He gently nudged her awake.

"Oh my God!"

Chase shushed her. They paused, but Leonardo did not move. He just kept snoring.

"We gotta get out of here!"

"Are they following you?"

"If they aren't, they will be."

Maddy started to gather her things and asked, "What happened to you?"

"Never mind that. I'll tell you when we get out of here." Chase continued to whisper, "We have to find the portal in the bell tower."

"Maybe it's not in the tower."

"Has to be. The portal's always in the highest building."

Maddy and Chase suddenly went very quiet. The snoring behind them had stopped. They looked. They listened. They waited.

No movements. No sounds. No rustling. Leonardo must still be asleep.

Chase squatted anxiously as Maddy put on her shoes. His eyes drifted up to the unfinished Mona Lisa. He thought how close he was to the most famous painting in the world. His Grandpa would have been proud. He was becoming an explorer, out seeing things in the world. That thought was quickly erased though. Mainly due to the fact that he was now a fugitive of the Florentine government and being hunted by Machiavelli's city militia.

Then Chase had an idea. "What if we go to another city and find another portal." He thought it was brilliant. Maddy did not.

"Are you sure there is another portal in the next city?"

Chase didn't. But he really didn't want to return to Florence. "I...maybe...there was one in New York."

"Yeah. But where should we go?"

Chase had no idea.

Maddy concluded, "I'd say we head back to Florence and find the portal that we think is there."

"We don't know there's a portal there."

"I think I do. I think if the portal is not in the bell tower than it has to be in the church."

Chase questioned Maddy's logic, "Really?"

"Yeah. When I was standing up there, I looked over at the dome. It was just as tall as the tower."

Chase was thinking as Maddy continued, "I think we should go back and try the cathedral. I think that's where the portal lies."

Chase sighed. "You know if the portal isn't there, we're doomed. They'll catch us for sure."

"We'll find it."

Chase wasn't as optimistic. "If we can even get in there..."

"We will." Maddy was resolved, "We have to get

into that church."

A voice came from behind them, "It won't work." They quickly tensed up. Leonardo had been listening. "At least, it will not be easy."

They both stared, waiting on the reason. "It's Sunday. There's Mass. And Machiavelli will be there."

Chase pleaded, "We can't wait. Troops will be here soon."

Maddy agreed, "Yeah, Leonardo. We have to go now."

"By the time you get to Florence, the city will be waking up."

They asked the old man, "How can we get into the basilica dome?"

Leonardo's eyes lit up. He leapt from his bed and grabbed a wood carving. It was a bird. He handed it to Chase. "You grow wings."

Chase's eyes popped open. *What does this old man mean?*

They reached the outskirts of the city without seeing one policeman. And that wasn't as easy as it may have sounded because each of the three carried various bulky materials with them. Chase had a bunch of wooden sticks. Twenty or thirty of them, about three inches in diameter and three or four feet long. They were very smooth and very straight, sanded and covered in a clear sealant. The rods were actually quite slippery and kept sliding against each other. Chase had to balance his load with every step he took.

Maddy carried a big pile of rope. Leonardo had piled it in her outreached arms so she didn't know how long it would reach if it were extended end to end but she estimated at least a hundred feet. Leonardo had a huge piece of linen, folded and folded again, draped over his back.

The kids knew nothing of his plan or the reason for the "part" they were lugging back into the city and straight into the arms of the city police force but Leonardo had been so convincing and so passionate that they couldn't say no. Even if this was the same man who had gotten Chase locked up in jail the day before. For some reason, they believed him and trusted his plan…whatever that was.

They trusted him as they snuck through the back alleys of Florence. They trusted him as they walked in the shadows of early morning. They trusted him as they tiptoed through streets they had not seen before. They trusted him until they arrived up at the back door of the Bell Tower.

"No, Leonardo. No. Not the Bell Tower, the Cathedral."

He nodded at Chase before continuing to jimmy the lock.

Chase pleaded a little louder. "The Cathedral of Santa Maria! Not the Bell Tower. We've been here. And it didn't work."

Leonardo nodded again and went right back to the lock.

Chase scowled at Maddy, "what's with this old man?" He turned back to Da Vinci and got a little louder, "SANTA MARIA! THE CHURCH."

Leonardo grabbed him by the arm, just like the officer did the night before, and pulled him around the western edge of the structure. People were already filing into the cathedral for the sunrise Mass. But that wasn't what stunned Chase. Most of the citizens of Florence would pay him no mind. What stunned Chase, was the troops lined up around the church. It was quite a display of power.

"Polizia."

Chase nodded in agreement as they ducked back behind the Bell Tower. Leonardo added another word for affect. "Potenza." He flexed his muscles when he did to make sure the translation was clear. Machiavelli had 'power.'

The three climbed the now familiar steps of the Bell Tower to the top floor. Careful not to be seen, they ducked and drooped as they began the construction of Leonardo's crazy flying machine.

First, they laid out the wooden sticks and began lashing them together into two large triangles. Then the linen was laid on top of each triangle, measured and cut. After the big piece became two, it was tied to the sticks. The ropes then made a harness-like pouch in the middle of the two triangles for the passenger. Chase and Maddy watched as Leonardo the engineer whipped the ropes around tying them off and lacing them back and through and over and under the wooden sticks that now looked like poles.

They thought they knew what they were doing next and tried to step in and help but Leonardo waved them away. He pointed to the roof, back at the two large triangles and back to the roof again. Then he gave his final instruction. They must be extremely quiet. Not a sound.

He had constructed most of the "wings" inside to

keep out of sight. Being on the roof for so long would have attracted attention. The kids found this out when they were secretly bringing the two wings to the rooftop. As they looked over, a few of the "Polizia" were stationed on the Basilica rooftop.

Chase asked Leonardo, "Why?"

"Signore Machiavelli expects war before he expects peace. Pisa or Bologna or the Medici could attack at anytime."

Careful again not to stand up straight, the three put the final touches on the wings. As Leonardo made the final tie downs, the kids finally realized what they were making.

"It's a hang glider!"

Maddy was right. And loud. Loud enough in her excitement to alert the guards across the town square, standing on the Basilica. They began yelling and pointing. Straight at the top of the Bell Tower.

It took ten seconds to get the attention of the policemen on the ground and another ten seconds to point out the potential threat. The screams sent the armed militia sprinting toward the Bell Tower.

Leonardo flung Chase into the harness and began to tie him in. As he did, he ripped off the backpack that was causing problems mounting the glider on his back. In the seconds that seemed like minutes, Chase was strapped in and lead to the edge of the tower. It was a long way down!

Leonardo steadied him and then offered his encouragement. "Saltare, Chasio, saltare."

Chase took the screams to mean he should jump and yet he hesitated, "What if I fall?"

Leonardo had an answer. "Get up and try again, boy. Get up and jump again!"

Chase stood statue still. It was a long way down.

"How do you steer this thing?"

"Like a bird. Now saltare!"

Chase did not move. He looked up, "Maddy, get over here."

She didn't move either. Leonardo warned, "No. Just you. This isn't built for two."

"I can't leave her."

"You're going to go back to jail soon!" Leonardo added.

Maddy chimed in, "Just jump, Chase."

"Not without you." He turned his back at Leonardo who was egging him on.

"Not without Maddy!"

Leonardo's shoulders dropped. "You ruin the calculations!"

Chase was stubborn. "I don't care. If they get her, they'll kill her."

Leonardo relented. "Fine!"

He started to unlace the harness for two when the shouts of the police grew louder.

Chase pushed the old man away, "There's no time!" He balanced on the edge, but almost lost his footing. "Whoa…"

He looked over at Maddy. His voice was forceful. "C'mon. This is our chance."

The police were close to reaching the top floor. One more set of stairs to the roof. Before Maddy hugged him for dear life around the chest, she threw the pack on her back. Chase looked over her shoulder at the four hundred foot drop. Maddy looked around Chase's arm at the police got to the roof.

"Go, Chase, go!"

He grabbed her and they jumped.

The hang glider went down…straight down. They weren't flying…they were falling!

"CHASE!"

"Hold on." Chase was trying to get his arms up but the glider was heavy. With all his might, he pushed his arms as high as he could over his head. The "wings" caught a little of the wind and they began to drift up. He pushed a little higher and they went a little higher.

Talking to himself, "OK, that works." Chase was beginning to get the science behind flying. Whether it was a little Nintendo DS logic or basic laws of physics, one just instinctually knew. He had straightened the glider out and turned it toward the Basilica.

On the ground, people looked up at the largest bird they'd ever seen. Behind him, the police watched in wonder and disbelief. Next to them, Leonardo cheered. Whether he cheered the kids or his invention, they would never know, but he screamed at the top of his lungs.

Chase was mastering the flying. Now for the next item of on-the-job training, stopping! The Basilica of Santa Maria was getting bigger and bigger. They were going faster and faster. A collision was about to occur.

"Maddy, hold on. This might hurt a little."

"What?"

"I said hold on!"

The best and most experienced hang glider could not have prevented hitting the cathedral. This was true. Because at this moment, Chase was the only hang glider the world had ever seen.

Avoiding the dome was impossible. The best he could do was aim for one of the windows and hopefully land inside and not smash against the stone-wall of the basilica dome.

His eyes darted back and forth until he spotted a window he knew he could hit. He kept the wings as steady as he could and tried to mimic the airplanes that landed on the runways back home. Keep the wings even and parallel to the ground and hopefully, just hopefully they would survive…to be caught by the police and tortured to death.

Chase hit his goal. He kept it steady and hit the window at a rapid pace. Luckily for Chase…and Maddy, he picked the right window. What he was about to learn is that a portal can be active either way you pass through it. This time, it was from the outside of the building, heading in.

The wings of the glider crashed against the side of the dome but the kids did not. They flew right through, disappearing like a bug on the windshield of a car. They had been transported to another time and they didn't see what was quickly called a miracle among the townspeople of Florence. They didn't see Machiavelli order every citizen to never speak of this event again or else face an evening of the strapaddo. And they didn't see a giggling Leonardo quickly pick up the broken wooden sticks, rope and linen and bounce home in joy and elation.

What the kids saw was red dirt...or clay to be exact. The hot red clay in which they landed in, face first. They sat up and dusted themselves off.

Chase spoke first, "Anything look familiar to you?"

Maddy scanned the landscape. Fields. Desolate fields of dirt and clay. And not a crop in sight. The bluest sky you could imagine and a nuclear hot sun in that sky.

When they turned around, a small country church stood, barely, behind them. Maddy looked around. "No...well, sort of. I haven't been here before but it sounds like something I heard about."

Chapter 15

"Heard about this place?"

Chase continued with his question, "Where?"

"From my Grandfather. He'd tell me stories of a place like this."

"Did he ever mention the heat?"

"It was one of the first things he'd talk about."

The kids were dripping sweat within minutes of landing in this new location. Without speaking, they both made their way to the huge pine tree near the front of the country church. The sun was out of their eyes but the heat still engulfed them.

"So where did your grandfather say this place was?"

"Alabama. It's where he grew up."

"Really?"

Chase thought a moment. "So you might have relatives around here?"

Maddy hadn't thought about that. "Maybe...I guess."

"Wanna look around?"

The first place they looked was the church. Outside, it was propped up off the ground with stumps of wood. The siding comprised of long unfinished pine, painted white but still weathered. Twinges of decay and rotting wood could be seen along the edges. The entire church was surrounded with a bed of pine needles, spread and raked in a rudimentary, but careful method of landscaping.

Inside, sparse would be an overstatement. A wood carved crucifix hung in the front, behind the dark stained pulpit. Pews were fashioned from split pine trees. There were no backs to the benches. They looked like old bleachers seats that could be found at the local high school. The walls were whitewashed and the thin, arching windows, three to each side, were opened to allow the flow of air. It didn't matter. Inside was as hot as the spot under the semi-shady pine.

The old floorboards creaked and whined with each step. This was worse than Grandpa Wally's second floor, Chase thought. There was no way a person could sneak into a packed church after the service had started without being heard.

And there was no way the kids could walk in the *empty* church without being heard. Today was just that type of situation. A door behind the altar slowly opened and a head peered back to see the visitors.

"May I help you, child?"

The elderly black minister was looking directly at Maddy.

"We're just trying to get out of the sun."

The minister answered her with a bible verse, "Revelation 16:8-9. And the fourth angel poured out his vial upon the sun; and power was given unto him to scorch men with fire."

He rose as he spoke and he entered the sanctuary, stopping when he noticed it wasn't just Maddy but a young white man as well. After a moment of looking Chase over, he continued with his quote, "And men were scorched with great heat, and blasphemed the name of God, which hath power over these plagues: and they repented not to give him glory."

Both the kids stared at him. Both their faces said the same thing: HUH? The minister saw this and dialed his rhetoric back. "You two, visiting someone in the area?"

Chase began, "Not really."

Maddy ended it. "Just passing through."

"I see. Well, welcome to Macon County, Alabama."

Maddy elbowed Chase. "I told you it reminded me of Alabama."

"What was that, young lady?"

"I was just telling him that this place reminded me of the place where my grandfather grew up."

The minister lit up, "Oh really? Where is he from?"

"Mitchell Crossroads."

"REALLY?! That's just up the road a spell!"

That shocked Maddy. "It is?"

"Yes, indeed. About a two-hour horse ride. About half a day on foot."

Maddy stood stunned. She was so close to the home of her ancestors. She sat on one of the pews and thought for a moment. Both men looked at her to see if she was OK. She was. Her head was moving a mile a minute...but in a good way. She had heard so many stories from her grandfather and now she was there. A place she never thought she'd see.

The minister interjected to break the silence, "Eatin' supper in a little while. Care to join me and my family?"

Chase looked to Maddy, who nodded quickly. He could tell this place was affecting his friend.

The kids sat around a small table in the little shack of a house. They were squished together with the other twelve members of the Minister's family. Kids and adults, they all shared a minimal meal of cornbread that could be dipped into a small amount of molasses. There was a little rice and okra in a stew-like gravy poured on top. It was spicy and it was served hot but somehow it actually seemed to cool them down. It may have seemed like a pauper's lunch, but it was the food of kings to the kids. And they inhaled it.

As the kids ate, the adults were speaking about the fields. They were facing a huge deadline to finish the picking. The crop needed to make it to market or the family would face a penalty.

Maddy had been listening more than eating. "Can we help?"

All of the adults craned their heads.

The Minister started to chuckle, "You really care to work up an appetite?"

Maddy clarified, "We would like to help out. To say thank you." She nudged Chase again who looked up from his cornbread and molasses. "Right, Chase?"

Chase agreed.

The blazing afternoon sun was back hitting their foreheads. Chase and Maddy were standing in the hot sun, in the hot air and in the hot dirt. The Minister looked over as the kids dripped from sweat, "This is the 40 acre and a mule we were promised."

The kids didn't understand so he continued, "This was the promise. From the government. They were going to give all slaves 40 acres and mule as payment for their treatment."

Another sharecropper, from another family, that also farmed that field walked by at the moment. He was a large man with a large scowl and he looked mean. He carried a number of tools in his hands. With those tools, he also had a rifle. His eyes were particularly focused on Chase. From that moment on Chase thought of him as the "Scowling Man."

Chase stood out no doubt. He was the only white kid in the field. Whether the Scowling Man was mad at Chase or just the world, either way, his snarl toward Chase was not welcoming.

The Minister defused the situation, "Let's get back to work. This cotton field isn't going to pick itself."

As the day wore on, Chase would continue to stand. Picking cotton was a very difficult job. A sack that draped over one shoulder would get heavier and heavier. It took a tremendous amount of back strength as the picker was bent over for a majority of the day. It also took a high pain threshold. Pulling cotton from the plant was difficult. The "cotton puff" or "cotton boll" was held to the plant by sharp bristles. Maddy and Chase learned quickly as their fingers were bleeding from the small cuts on each and every finger.

Every time Chase stood and stretched, he would look over the field. And it seemed like every time he would, the Scowling Man was looking straight at him. Chase and Maddy weren't as efficient, nor as strong, as the sharecropping families and had to periodically rest. They had to get out of the sun. That meant finding a shade tree near the edge of the fields.

While resting, Chase shared with Maddy his thoughts about his newest enemy. She scoffed, saying he was imagining things.

Chase wouldn't stop, "I heard him whisper 'Who's the white boy?'"

"That doesn't mean he's mad at you."

"He keeps staring at me."

"I'm tired of it." Chase looked up and saw the Scowling Man staring at him. "See."

Maddy looked, but she wasn't seeing what her traveling friend was seeing. Chase grew tired of the stare and gave him back a snarl. The Scowling Man leaned down and picked up his rifle, starting toward Chase. Fear shot through Chase's body. *He's coming over to shoot me!* Chase tried to jump to his feet.

The Scowling Man yelled at Chase. "Don't move!"

But Chase backed up even more.

"DON'T MOVE, BOY!"

He raised the rifle, cocking in one motion, aimed and fired. The bullet whizzed by Chase's ear. Chase dove to his right, too late to avoid the bullet but his reaction to being shot at, nonetheless. Chase bounced back up from the dirt field to look back at the man. He wasn't shot. Not in the least. But he thought he was going to have to dodge another bullet. He wasn't. The man wasn't looking at Chase but rather at his kill. A headless cottonmouth snake lay dead on the ground, just feet from Chase.

"I...I...didn't even know he was behind me."

"That was his plan. Southern hospitality doesn't extend to southern creatures."

Chase stared. The shock was sinking in. The old man picked up the snake and handed him to Chase. "Take this back to the house. Momma can make a fine stew out of that."

"Huh?"

"Then sit down for a while. You look like you've seen the devil, boy."

Chase shuffled away thinking: *I almost got shot!* After the shock wore off, he looked down at his hand to see a dead snake. He shuttered and threw it into the brush along the side of the road.

"What are you doing?!" Maddy screamed.

"I AM NOT EATING THAT!"

"Maybe you won't, but they will."

Chase couldn't believe she was saying that.

"You obviously don't know what's it's like to not have money."

Chase and Maddy got back to the house...with the snake in very quick time. When they did, another man had arrived just after the time they did. He was a young black man with a large pull cart. The lanky gentleman set it down before checking the row of shacks, looking for someone to appear. No one was at the house, so he sat on a tree stump and opened a book. Chase and Maddy watched him read for a few minutes before offering him some information.

"They're still in the fields."

The young gentleman nodded and returned to his book.

"Probably will be for awhile."

"I figured. They usually return around dusk. Just got here a little early."

"Are you hoping to sell something?"

"Nope." Again he went back to reading.

Maddy was too curious...and a little bored so she ventured over to him.

"What are you reading?"

"It's called the Codex Leicester."

"Oh. What's it about?"

"Well, I guess I'd call it an illustration of the link between art and science and the creativity of the scientific process."

Maddy nodded like she knew what he was talking about,

"You've heard of it?"

"No," but quickly added to keep up appearances, "sounds interesting. Who wrote it?"

"Who?! Who you ask?"

"I did. That is what I asked."

"It was written by Leonardo da Vinci."

"da Vinci? I know him."

"So you've read his work?"

"No. I—never mind." Maddy couldn't go into it. She looked at Chase who was hoping she wouldn't. She gave him a "I know!" glare back. Maddy turned back to the gentleman, "What do these people need with da Vinci?"

"Everything. Wait! These people?"

"Yeah, these people are sharecroppers. They can barely pay for food. They don't need da Vinci."

"Not so fast. I disagree with you completely."

Maddy's face scrunched.

"This book covers a variety of subjects, flight, weaponry, musical instruments, mathematics, botany…"

"Weaponry and botany? What do they have in common?"

"Judging by that headless cottonmouth you walked up here with, someone used weaponry to decapitate it."

"Ok. But what about botany?"

"Can I assume you were standing in or near a field of cotton when that killing took place?"

Maddy got his point. She didn't acknowledge it, but she got it. "So who are you?"

"My name is George."

"George, are you here to make sure the field is fully ginned?"

"Nope."

She was a little shocked, "You're not?"

"Nope."

"So you're not here about the cotton?"

"I didn't say that."

"So you are here about the cotton?"

"In a way."

"What does that mean?" she asked.

George rose from his seat and guided Maddy to the clearing that looked out over the fields. "What do you see?"

"Fields."

"Fields of what?"

"Cotton."

"Good. Cotton and what else?"

"Ahh…" She wanted to get this right but she didn't have the answer. "Well…it all looks the same."

George quickly interjected, "Exactly! Cotton and cotton and more cotton."

"Ok."

"And why do you think cotton is all that is grown here?"

"…because it grows well."

"Used to."

"But it looks like it still does."

"If you read histories of Macon County, you would discover that cotton plants were 5% taller ten years ago. 10% taller twenty years ago. What does that tell you?"

"They're shrinking. The plants are shrinking."

"Yes. And you know why?"

"Why?"

"Because the agricultural monoculture of cotton depletes the soil."

"Agricultural monoculture?"

"It's the process of only growing one crop in a field year after year. Certain plants like cotton take certain nutrients from the soil whereas corn or wheat or soybeans take different nutrients from the soil."

Maddy was enthralled.

"But in that same vein, those same plants put other things back into the soil. It's a theory called crop rotation."

"You want them to plant different crops?"

"Yes."

"Which one's?"

"Anything different would be better than cotton, but I have one that would be the best."

"Which crop would be the best?"

"Peanuts."

Chapter 16

"Peanuts?"

"Yes. I want them to plant peanuts."

"Why?"

George looked her in the eyes. "You want to see?"

She nodded.

"Then you need to come to my lab."

"Where?"

"Tuskegee."

"Isn't that a school?"

"Well, technically it is an Institute."

She turned back to Chase who was still staring at the headless snake. "C'mon Chase, we're going to college."

"I'm still not going to eat that."

George interjected, "Back on campus, I've got something better to eat than a cottonmouth snake."

Chase eagerly agreed to follow.

Tuskegee rose over the fields in front of them. Majestic buildings for this area. There were several classroom buildings, a chapel, administration building as well as student dormitories. Red brick and wood. As active educational campus as seen all over the country.

"This was an old plantation." George proudly exclaimed.

"And now it's a college?"

"It was abandoned and our president, Dr. Washington, thought it could be our home."

George told them that each and every building on the grounds were built or rebuilt by the students...using their hands. "And they made sure they built them right."

When Maddy asked what that meant, he replied, "These buildings were going to be handed down to future students. If the structure and the foundation of a building was not sound, didn't that mean the school was not either?"

Chase wasn't listening closely but Maddy was. "George, what's your job?"

"I work with farmers."

"Doing what?"

"Improving the lot of 'the man farthest down.'"

Their faces showed confusion.

"The poor, one-horse farmer at the mercy of the

market and chained to land exhausted by cotton. Like I said before, get 'em off of cotton and into peanuts."

Maddy asked how.

"Come with me and I'll show you."

George walked them through the halls of the science building and toward his laboratory. The white washed walls held chalkboards and bulletin boards with his handwritten notes and ideas.

"We need to devise practical farming methods for this kind of farmer. I wanted to coax them away from cotton to such soil-enhancing, protein-rich crops as soybeans and peanuts and to teach them self-sufficiency and conservation."

Chase stared off in the distance. He was not thrilled to be on this tour, especially one so technical and scientific. Maddy, however, kept asking George question after question. The scientist in her was bursting out.

George told her he might achieve this through educational visits to the fields. "I gotta be out there talking to them. Hearing what they say and seeing what they see. I have to catch myself because I'd just as soon spend the whole day in here, running experiments." Chase was thinking he'd like to be back in the field, because this tour was getting boring!

They had arrived at his laboratory. It looked like the home of a mad scientist. Tubes went to beakers and back to hollow glass balls containing various liquids. Things were bubbling and dripping and sitting and waiting for the scientist to return. There were notebooks next to each of the experiments on each of the four long lab tables. It was cluttered, stacked and messy. It looked like he'd been conducting experiments for years. But George told them he just moved into this lab last week.

Maddy had a quick assessment. "This looks like Edison's lab." Chase quickly agreed.

George overheard. "What did you say?"

Maddy told him that she and Chase had visited Thomas Edison's laboratory in New Jersey and it looked very similar.

When George heard this, a huge smile appeared on his face. He looked like a kid on Christmas morning.

"I like the sound of that."

Both kids wondered why, but George didn't hear them. He was floating around the room, his head in the clouds thinking that his research techniques were one and the same with the world famous Thomas Edison. He stopped mid-float and turned to his visitors, "Oh, that reminds me." George disappeared into the side room, returning with a newspaper in hand. "Speaking of Edison, this was left behind by a traveling professor. You should read this article."

It was a New York Times newspaper from April 24th with a headline reading:

EDISON'S VITASCOPE CHEERED. "Projecting Kinetoscope" Exhibited for First Time at Koster and Bial's. The ingenious inventor's latest toy is a projection of his kinetoscope figures in stereopticon fashion on a white screen in a darkened hall. In the center of the balcony of the big music hall is a curious object, which looks from below like the double turret of a big monitor. The moving figures are about half-life size.

Both kids smiled...beamed...but said nothing. They didn't have to brag...or really read the article. They were there!

As the kids read the article, George took a spoon from the lab table and dipped it into a bowl, "Here, try this."

Maddy took a bite of the light brown paste.

"What do you think?" George asked.

She smiled. "Good."

George took another spoon, handing the same to Chase. He took a bite.

"Well…?"

Chase wasn't impressed and his answer was very nonchalant, "Kinda bland peanut butter."

George was shocked. "Bland?"

"Yeah, bland."

George was still stunned, "Well…"

"Peanut butter should be sweeter." Chase offered.

"Well, it's a work in progress."

"Not bad, just needs to be a little sweeter." Chase was slightly distracted and returned his eyes to the newspaper. "Is this the date?"

George said no. That was last spring.

"What's the date today?"

"October 15th."

Maddy's head was elsewhere. She was still eating the peanut butter. "So this is why you want the farmers to grow peanuts?"

"One of many reasons. Peanuts can give them more than just peanut butter."

"Like what?"

"Peanut milk, peanut oil, relish, paste, meat

substitutes…well, I think the peanut's uses are endless."

Then Chase chimed in, "And you're going to do all of that?"

"I'm going to try. That's why they brought me in as the head of the agricultural department."

"How long have you been here, George?"

"Couple of months."

Later in the evening, George and the kids sat outside on the building steps, each with another spoon of his peanut butter, watching the sun go down over the tall southern pines. Maddy peppered George with questions as Chase scanned the buildings of the campus.

He was handed the spoon. And it was full of another glop of peanut butter. He hesitated but took another taste. It still wasn't his favorite but it sure was better than cottonmouth snake so he ate it.

"Is this _your_ invention?"

"Yes…well, this particular composition. But I guess I must make improvements."

"No, I mean, are you the man who invented peanut butter?"

"Well…maybe not the entire concept but this recipe certainly is. I've heard of some other men creating something like it but I don't know for sure."

The businessman in Chase came out, "If you get it to the stores first, you'll make a lot of money with it."

George didn't seem that interested in Chase's advice. "Food is a gift from God. It isn't mine from which to profit. I'd rather make sure people didn't go hungry."

"Whatever. I'm just saying you could make a lot of

money and feed a lot more people if you owned a peanut butter company."

"Chase, he's a scientist, not a businessman!"

"Why can't he be both? Edison is."

Maddy was quiet. Chase had got her with that one.

"Children, let's not fight about it. Maddy is right. I am not a businessman. I'm only a scientist. Try as I might, I just don't see the world for the money it could make me. I don't make much but I don't spend much. It's one of my eight cardinal rules: *Take your share of the world and let others take theirs.*"

"What are the others?" Chase asked.

George reached into his pants pocket and handed him a small handwritten card. Chase read the other seven:

Be clean both inside and out.

Lose, if need be, without squealing.

Win without bragging.

Always be considerate of women,
children, and older people.

Be too brave to lie.

Be too generous to cheat.

Neither look up to the rich, nor down on the poor.

George waited until Chase had finished. "You can keep that. I know them by heart."

Chase slid it into his pocket. "Thanks."

"Well kids, the Jesup wagon won't push itself tomorrow morning. It's my bed time."

"Jesup wagon?"

"My cart. The one I take around the county to visiting the farmers."

Maddy added, "The man farthest down?"

George nodded and went to bed but not before showing the kids an empty room where they could spend the night.

As they both lay quietly in the dormitory beds, Chase broke the silence. "Doesn't it feel like we should be running?"

Maddy quickly shot back. "No, not at all."

"Really? I mean, we've been here for almost a day and no one's chasing us and we're not chasing anyone."

Maddy smiled, "That snake had you in its sights."

"Yeah. That creeped me out." Chase paused briefly, "And then they thought I was going to have to eat it! Can you believe that?!"

Maddy giggled.

"I need a good cheeseburger...or maybe some more of that spaghetti..."

Again Maddy laughed.

Chase was thinking of the last meal he had before he left Grandpa Wally's farmhouse. "Boy, I want to go home."

Now Maddy was silent.

"Don't you?"

Maddy was drifting off to sleep but softly added, "No...this feels like home."

Chase's eyes popped open in the darkness. He

couldn't sleep. Maddy had no problem. That's why it took him a while to get her awake.

"Maddy, we gotta find the portal."

Still half asleep, "It's gotta be in the chapel."

"How do you know?"

"I don't but I'll ask George."

"Well, go now." Chase urged.

She tried to roll over. "In the morning."

"Ask him now."

"No. He's asleep."

"Then, let's go investigate now."

"Why?"

"Less people are out."

Maddy hemmed and hawed. She was comfortable. She was lying down and tired from all the chaos of the last few days. And when Chase hovered inches above her, she pulled the sheet over her head. It didn't stop Chase. He pleaded. And he didn't stop.

Frustrated, "Fine!"

Getting across campus was quick. The small chapel sat in the middle of campus, dark and quiet. They crept up the five steps that led to the front door and slowly opened the door. The entire building was made of wood, the creakiest wood in the world if you asked Chase. Even more than the country church. But with the campus so quiet, any noise they made seemed to echo over the whole college.

Minutes later, they searched the doors and windows for the sun symbol. But in the darkness, they were not successful.

Chase reluctantly admitted, "Maybe we *should* have waited until morning."

Now Maddy was more frustrated, "You couldn't have told me that earlier? Like when I was still in bed!"

"I didn't know it was going to be so hard!"

"What's the rush anyway?"

That irritated Chase, "My Grandpa?! I mean, at least you're back in your time."

Maddy was quiet until Chase looked over at him. "I know...I've been thinking about that since we got here."

"I'm just tired of this. I'm tired and want to get home."

"OK," Maddy sympathetically answered. "Let's keep looking."

They searched the windows and doors again. This time Chase used his small flashlight to shine around each opening. After another hour of looking they were stumped.

"Are you sure this is the tallest building on campus?"

"No. But it looked like it."

"We've looked everywhere."

Chase agreed. They had. Then something popped in Maddy's head. "What about under the chapel?"

"What do you mean?"

"I mean, the portal could be anywhere, right?"

"Yeah."

"And when we found the one in New York, it was more like a window, right?"

Chase again said yes.

"And in London, it was the main door."

"Yeah."

Maddy continued, "Florence was a really high window…"

"So you think it might be a really low window here?"

"I'm just saying, anything can be a portal."

Chase was already out the door.

By the time Maddy arrived outside, Chase was investigating the foundation of the chapel. It was built off the ground, but a person couldn't see under the church. The foundation was covered with wood planks, painted the same as the chapel walls.

Chase searched one side and Maddy searched the other. The moon shone down, but it was still dark. Maddy had found a small vertical seam in the wood and thought it might be a portal. She kept trying to pull it out but she was having a devil of a problem. Her fingers were wedged into the seam but it was just not coming loose. That did not stop her.

AAAAAGGGGHHHHH!

What stopped her was a blood-curdling scream from the other side. She bolted to the other side to see Chase standing frozen a few feet away from the side of the chapel.

"What? Chase, what is it?" A few more steps and she didn't need to hear his answer. Of course, he was frozen and not talking anyway. He was staring straight into the eyes of another cottonmouth, a reared up snake with anger in its hiss. This hiss was so loud that if Chase's scream didn't wake up the campus, this hiss would.

Maddy's eyes went from the snake to Chase and back to the snake. She looked above the three foot by three foot opening that led under the chapel. Carved into the wood was a small but very visible sun symbol. This was the portal and it was being guarded.

"Chase."

He'd didn't answer.

She was a little louder, "Chase!"

Still nothing from him.

"CHASE!"

His stare snapped and he looked over to Maddy. "You know how much I hate snakes?"

"He didn't bite you, did he?"

Chase shook his head no.

"That's good."

"We have to move it."

Maddy partially agreed, "OK…"

For the next hour, they poked and prodded with a stick. They threw stones and they threw rocks but that snake just got angrier and angrier and hissed louder and louder but never moved.

The kids took a break. They had run out of ideas, hoping that maybe if they left it alone, it would move on its own. It didn't.

When the streams of daylight began to appear, the kids saw why. It was a snake in the process of giving birth. There was no way the mother snake would move.

"What do we do?"

Maddy corrected him, "You mean you."

Chase's head whipped away from looking at the chapel and directly into Maddy's eyes. "WHAT?!"

"I'm not going with you this time."

"Maddy!"

"I'm sorry, Chase, but I can't."

"Why?"

"Like you said, I'm back in my time. It's only a few months different than when we left."

Chase was silent...and hurt.

"Chase, don't be that way. I wasn't supposed to be on this trip anyway."

"You don't know that. Maybe I was supposed to find you."

"Maybe. But now, I'm home...or at least close."

"New Jersey is your home."

"But this is my grandfather's home. His boyhood home. And I can stay here. And meet some of my relatives."

"Don't you want to see your mom again...and your Grandpa?!"

"I can. I can work with George and make some money and take the train home in a few months."

"But—"

"—Chase, maybe this is the end of my trip. I mean, I could go to school here...at a black college. We don't have those in New Jersey."

As Maddy kept talking, Chase's shoulders slumped down farther and farther. Everything she was saying made sense. And everything she said made him think she was in the right place.

"Chase, you are my friend and always will be. And I hope we cross paths when we are older but I just have this feeling deep in my heart that I am supposed to be right here, right now."

Chase was getting sad. He didn't want to let her see his face because he felt like he might tear up a little.

"Fine. I'll go ahead and leave you here."

"Chase, don't be mad. This has been the coolest couple of days I have ever had. And that's because of you."

It was sinking into Chase's brain.

"Just think if you found your grandfather. Don't you think you'd stop looking for a portal and just enjoy the place you were."

"I guess..."

"Well here...in Tuskegee. I found my grandfather...or his old home. And it's where I'm supposed to be."

"Ok." Chase finally agreed with her. "You're right." Then he added, "but we should get together again someday."

"We will!" She beamed. "If you come find me, you're the time traveler!"

"I will. I promise."

They hugged. Chase couldn't believe he was hugging a girl but then he got over it and gave his friend a tighter squeeze. His eyes looked up as they broke the embrace. His eyes were focused on the portal and the cottonmouth that guarded it.

"That momma ain't moving, is she?

"I don't think so."

"What should I do?"

"I think you should just jump."

"ARE YOU CRAZY?! JUMP TOWARD A SNAKE?!"

"You won't reach the snake. You'll fall through the

portal. It'll shoot you into another world and the snake will stay under the chapel at Tuskegee."

Chase stopped to ponder. Maybe she was right. Then again… "What if that isn't right?"

"It is." Maddy sounded confident. "Just like Leonardo said, "Saltare, Chasio! Saltare! And if it doesn't work, get up and jump again!"

"But that snake could kill me."

"It won't. It's on the other side of the portal. Remember the hang glider didn't come with us when we landed here."

Chase's face changed. That was true. The hang glider did not follow them into the portal. They flew through the portal alone.

A lot of things raced through Chase's brain and the last thing was the word: OK.

Chase stood twenty feet back from the portal. He aimed himself at the open door…right at the cottonmouth. Maddy stood a few away from the portal but to the side. She watched quietly as Chase readied himself for the jump. They had hugged and said goodbye once more. She had coached him into making this leap. He had backed away again, but she psyched him back to bravery.

The final trick she used was to shield his face with his backpack so he couldn't see the snake. This proved to be the wisest advice she had. It would protect him from a strike if this wasn't the portal, plus it blocked the very embodiment of his fear. How could he be scared if he couldn't see the snake? So there Chase stood, backpack raised in front of him, getting prepared to jump into another world.

"You can do this, Chase."

He nodded. Then stood still. No time like now he thought. Finally, when he was more tired of waiting than being scared, he took his first step. Then another and another. He ran. Backpack raised. Heart pumping. Snake hissing. Chase running.

Seconds later, he hit the portal. And it _was_ the portal. Maddy was right. Chase was propelled somewhere else in time. Maddy stood there alone. When she leaned over to investigate further, she saw nothing. No Chase. No backpack...and no snake.

Chapter 17

"Where's the snake?"

Maddy thought that. Even said it to herself. But there was nothing she could do. She placed the door back over the portal and walked away, thinking...hoping that Chase was OK.

Chase pulled the straw from his clothes and hair and his shoes. He had landed in a huge pile of it...in a barn. It was dark and smelt like fresh horses. Not very pleasant! As he pulled himself together in the quiet farm setting, he heard something. It was a hiss.

Chase's eyes popped open. He jumped ten feet in the air. Clinging to his backpack, fangs puncturing it deep, was that cottonmouth. Chase grabbed the first thing he could find, which was a shovel and whacked at the snake. It released its death bite and slithered away under the hay. Chase grabbed the backpack and ran toward the barn door. To get there, he had to push past the horses, horses that were freaked out by his sudden arrival. He tried to squeeze between past them and toward the moonlight that streamed through the cracks of the barn but they were too spooked. Rising up on their hind legs, they would easily crush Chase if he tried to run past them. He stopped.

Chase had learned long ago from his Grandpa, and the crazy ride through New York City, how to calm horses. He had to let them get it out of their system. When they calmed, he would put his hand on them and talk in a soothing manner and they would eventually mellow enough to let him pass. Of course, Chase wasn't about to keep his feet on the ground, not with that cottonmouth somewhere nearby. He jumped up on the side of the barn and held on to the exposed two-by-fours that formed the inside walls. When the horses finally calmed down, Chase pushed the small corral gate open. He rounded the corner of the barn and saw a familiar sight.

WHOA! He was home…or at least Grandpa's home. The barn he had arrived in, was Grandpa Wally's! Man, that was cool. He was back and now he could rest and relax. He was sure his Mom and Dad were worried but now they could calm down, just like the horses. Chase started up the hill when he thought his eyes might be deceiving him. The old farmhouse looked a little different. Not as big…and neither were the trees. And as he looked back, the railing looked brand new. He took a few more steps up the hill and noticed a hole where the fallout shelter used to be. It looked like fresh dirt. Chase wondered if his parents had discovered the source of the portal and dug it up so no one else would ever jump from time to time again. *How did they figure it out? Maybe Mom knew? Maybe Grandpa had told her and she figured it out? Maybe Grandpa was back!*

No matter, Chase thought. As long as he was back and Grandpa was back, it would make for a great story. A story not many would ever believe, but a great story nonetheless.

Chase could barely see the back door as clouds had floated in front of the moon. The wind began to pick up. A storm must be rolling in. It wasn't cold, far from it. It was very warm, even muggy. *Oh, that bed would feel good.* Chase had been sleeping in chairs, on the floor and in any little nook or cranny he could find since this adventure had begun. Now, he'd have a good night's sleep and a huge breakfast in the morning and all would be right. And tomorrow he would be asking for more spaghetti…or a cheeseburger…or *good* peanut butter!

He bounded up the porch steps and toward the front door. He noticed that things had changed. The old swing seat was not there. And the screen door looked brand new. Mom and Dad must have been busy while he was gone, Chase thought. Busy with repairs when they weren't out looking for Grandpa….WAIT! They must have found him! Chase ran inside.

He stopped again. The living room had changed too. It was so clean. No boxes. No piles of papers. No stacks of books. The house even smelt different. *Boy, Mom must have been on a tear.* When she got after him to clean his room back in New York, there was no stopping her until he did it. *Grandpa must be wishing she would be going home soon.* But he could worry about that tomorrow, now it was time to see his parents and go to bed.

As he neared the top of the steps, he thought about waking his parents to tell them he was back. But he figured they were already asleep. Plus, he was tired. It could wait until morning.

He crept down the hallway, slightly confused. The floors didn't creak as much as they had when he had snuck out. And some of the furniture had changed. The old grandfather clock was still at the end of the hall but the thin table with all the pictures was gone. That's funny he thought. Then again, he didn't really care so why worry about it.

Chase pushed open his bedroom door to find the furniture hadn't changed here. Nope. Still the same. Same dresser. Same desk. Same chair. Bed in the same place. Even some sketches on the dresser. Right where he left them. He whipped off his backpack. Popped off his Nikes and threw his sweatshirt over the bedpost. Time to crash. He sat down and was about to swing his legs under the covers when he heard something.

Chase froze. That something he heard was breathing. He knew it wasn't the snake but his nerves were on edge after the last few hours. His left hand began to pat the bed. There was someone there. He sprang up. So did the person in the bed. Both questioning simultaneously. Both asking for the same person: Mom? Then the voice registered and they asked again: Dad?!

A second later a beam of light hit Chase in the face. He held up his hands to block the light. He took a step to the left. The light followed him. He took a step to the right. The beam hit him again.

"Stop, would ya?"

"Who are you?"

Asking the same but more annoyed, "*Who are you*?!

"Wallace."

"Wallace?"

"Yeah."

"Wallace, you're in my bed."

"This is my bed. Has been ever since I was born."

"Sorry dude, but this is my Grandpa's house and I would have known if he had a boy living with him."

"This is my room. See." With this, the beam finally left Chase's face and moved to various items in the room.

"That's my drawing. That's my radio. Those are my clothes in the closet and that's my poster!"

The beam was now focused on the poster on the wall. A movie poster...of Gunga Din. The classic adventure starring Cary Grant and Douglas Fairbanks and Victor McLaglen. Three guys Chase had never heard of except for the fact that he had seen this poster for years and years as he lay in that bed, unable to sleep. His head was filled with stories of adventure just like the one portrayed in the movie.

"That's been here for years."

"I just got it." And the beam returned to Chase's face.

But as it did, the beam passed by something that caught Chase's eye. "Hey, wait, shine that back a second."

"Huh?"

"Shine your light back on the wall."

Wallace obliged. He shone the light at the poster.

"No, over here." The boy in the bed followed the sound of Chase's voice. On the far wall, the light found the object of Chase's curiosity. It was a calendar. A calendar that showed the month of May. May _1956_.

Chase turned around and looked into the light. Then he took three steps toward the door. The beam from the flashlight did not matter anymore because Chase found the light switch and flicked it. Now, Chase looked at the other boy. Minus the different colored hair, he could have been looking at his brother…or maybe himself. It was crazy and creepy and about the last thing Chase expected to see. He turned and sprinted out of the room, down the stairs and into the basement. This time he didn't care about furniture, smells or noise. He wanted to get to the fallout shelter as soon as possible.

Chase knew the way, so this wasn't hard. The house hadn't changed…or rather the house had stayed the same from 1956 to 2010. The direct route to the basement was only different in that the kitchen table and chairs were slightly askew. Other than that, Chase juked and jived and thumped loudly down the basement steps. He took the hard left with no reservations and ran down the same dirt hallway that sent him on this adventure. He ran toward the shelter doors. He was going to jump to another time. And soon. Before he "influenced or infected" this time and the boy upstairs.

Only, when Chase reached the shelter doors, they weren't there. Actually, nothing was there. It was just a hole. A hole of fresh dirt and nothing else. No room with supplies. No steel frame. No sun above the non-existent frame. Nothing but the wind. And the clouds. And the partial moonlight.

It didn't work. He didn't get blasted into the past. He didn't jump to another time. He didn't get transported. He just stood on the top of a dirt mound. Staring.

"What's your problem?"

Chase turned around to see Wallace. Chase couldn't answer. He just fell down, landing his rear in the dirt, his head shaking.

"I don't know…"

"Know what?"

"…if I can tell you."

"Tell me what?"

"About the…"

Wallace looked at him for the next words.

"Let's just say that we're going to know each other in the future."

"How do you know that?"

"Because…I know things."

Wallace was confused and Chase's words didn't seem to help. "What do you know?"

Chase shook his head. He didn't want questions right now.

Wallace wasn't one to stop, "Who are you again?"

Chase looked back, figuring he was going to have to answer when he noticed Wallace shivering uncontrollably. It was a little windy but not uncomfortable by any means. "How come you're so cold?"

"I've been sick lately. First a fever, then the chills. Then more chills and back to the fever again."

"You should be in bed."

"I was. Until some stranger woke me up."

"Sorry. I thought I was somewhere else. A place that looked like this place."

"Really? There's another place that looks like my house?"

"Ah...yeah. Kind of."

"Where?"

"Couple of counties over."

"Wait, you said kind of. What do you mean?"

"In a few years." Chase mumbled.

Wallace scrunched his face, "Huh?"

"Never mind."

As Chase said that, a light clicked on in the second floor window. The window that was in Wallace's room. A face appeared in the window. It was Wallace's mother.

"Wallace?! What are you doing outside at this time of night?! You're sick!"

"I was just talking to this boy."

Wallace's mother looked around the entire lawn. There was no one standing there but Wallace himself. "Now you're seeing things?!" She leaned back inside and yelled to her husband, "Now, he's delusional. I told you we should have called the doctor this afternoon."

Wallace felt he had to defend himself, "I'm not delusional! I'm not seeing things!"

"Get up here this minute and back into bed!"

Wallace did as he was told. He wasn't delusional. There was a boy. At least, he kept mumbling that, but even he scanned the lawn and saw nobody. Still, he went inside knowing he wasn't crazy.

Chase had tucked himself inside the hole that would soon become the entrance to the fallout shelter. He was deep in the hole and couldn't have been seen unless someone jumped down in. He hung in the dark shadows. He did not want to be seen. He needed time to think. *This time jump was really screwy...how was he going to get out of this? AND THAT WAS HIS GRANDPA! As a boy! His Grandpa! Grandpa Wally! At his age! That made this beyond screwy.*

Then Chase's mind raced to other questions and thoughts. Maybe his Grandpa, even as a boy, had the answers on how to get home? But maybe he didn't and if he didn't, Chase might screw things up in the time travel system by telling the young Grandpa Wally. Then he might never get home!

The older Grandpa Wally said tell no one. But maybe he could tell the younger version. He hadn't really told anyone else...well, Maddy but he didn't tell her. She just got caught up with him and jumped accidentally. And he mentioned a few things to Aristotle, but not *every*thing. Just enough to get out of Athens. And I'm sure da Vinci and Machiavelli and the entire Florence city-state police force was a little confused when two kids just disappeared but he really couldn't do anything about that right now.

Plus, <u>this</u> was Grandpa Wally. And this was where he first entered the time travel system. This could really affect everything if he said or knew too much or did too much, too early. Chase may never get home. Ever. Maybe there would never be a time travel system and if there were no system, there was no way home. He would be stuck in some alternative world forever.

Chase was confused and tired and overwhelmed. He had no idea what to do. He just wanted to hide and scream and yell and curse and maybe, although he'd never admit to it, maybe cry just a little.

But all those thoughts disappeared when he heard the worst sound in the world. It wasn't thunder. Or lightning. It wasn't someone behind him asking him who he was. Or the sound of a shotgun being loaded or the hammer of a pistol being cocked back. It wasn't the sound of the Florence police chasing him. Or the growl of Jack the Ripper coming at him. Nope. The worst sound in the world to Chase was the sound of hissing. And hissing that was getting louder and louder.

Chase peeked up over the dirt pile he had just dove behind and looked face to face with his time traveling nemesis. The cottonmouth has slithered from the barn, through the grass, and toward the hole in which Chase was standing.

As she slithered up, Chase edged back. He was forced back deeper in the hole and inside the basement of the house. He didn't want to go back inside, but he definitely didn't want to tussle with that snake.

Inside the basement, Chase began his search for the sun symbol and his portal out of this twilight zone. First, the basement, to no luck. Then he moved to the first floor and came up just as empty-handed. Sneaking around, Chase went through every room in the entire house but two: Wallace's and his parents. He stood in the hallway. One to his left. One to his right.

Either choice is his only one. There is no way he could sneak through one and get a chance at the other. He had to make a choice.

The silence was broken when he heard a little hum of music. It was coming from Wallace's room. When Chase opened the door, Wallace sat in the dark, listening to an annoying song on the radio. It was some sort of big band, swing type of song. It was the kind of song that would put Chase to sleep if he had to listen to it for any length of time. The flashlight hit him right in the eyes. Chase put his finger to his mouth in a sign to keep quiet.

"I knew you were real."

Chase nodded. "What are you listening to?"

"Marconi's genius."

"Is that a band?"

"No. It's the radio."

"Marconi?"

"Invented by Guglielmo Marconi. In Bologna, Italy. 1894."

"I see. OK. I need your help." Wallace studied this foreigner standing in his room. Chase admitted to Wallace that he was sorry for hanging him out in the wind but it was best that no one else knew he was there. When Wallace asked why, Chase made a split second decision in self-defense. Or preservation.

"I'm going to tell you a few things that may seem crazy but like I said, I need your help."

"You're from the future."

Chase was blown away. "How…?"

"I'm kidding. It's just all the books I've been reading."

"The books?"

Wallace pulled the books off the nightstand, flashing his light on the covers. Chase looked through the titles: *Around the World in Eighty Days* and *Twenty Thousand Leagues Under the Sea*, by Jules Verne, *Looking Backward* by Edward Bellamy and *The Time Machine* by H.G. Wells.

"You're really into these kind of books, huh?"

"I think time travel is the next great invention."

"Really? When?"

"Who knows?"

"And who's going to be the person...?"

"I don't know but with minds like Einstein and Marconi laying the groundwork...and Oppenheimer and Sakharov and their advances with nuclear fusion. And the —"

Chase interrupted, " — wait, wait, Oppenheimer. Is that the guy who created the atomic bomb?"

"Well, yes."

"And because of that you're putting in that shelter in the basement."

Wallace laughed. "Yeah. Sort of."

Chase asked what he meant by "Sort of."

"That shelter isn't going to protect us from anything. I mean, I guess maybe from some radioactive rays that would potentially reach us here but that's only if Minneapolis was a target of the Russians. Any direct hit from a nuclear bomb and we'd be -"

" — flat as a pancake?"

"Flatter."

"And the Russians want to bomb us?"

"If you read the papers. But I kinda think it could just be a lot of bluster from both sides."

"What makes you say that?"

"M.A.D." From the look on Chase's face, he had no idea what Wallace was talking about. "Mutually Assured Destruction. If one bombs, the other bombs and everyone dies."

"You sure know a lot for a kid who is…"

"13."

Chase was more amazed. "You're 13 and reading about atomic bombs and nuclear weapons?"

Wallace went on to explain how he wasn't looking at these discoveries and inventions and the pain and destruction they could create but how, if harnessed, they could be used for amazing opportunities like time travel. He then threw terms like wormholes and space/time continuums, induced gravity and some idea that two identical universes may have been created by the Big Bang and they lay upon each other like two sheets.

Halfway through his lecture, Wallace lost Chase. The topics Wallace was explaining were over Chase's head. But it did trigger two thoughts in Chase's brain. The first was how, even at 13 years old, his grandfather was the smartest guy he knew. The second thing that popped in his head was simple. He loved listening to his grandfather, no matter what he was talking about, no matter how much he got or didn't get, listening to his grandpa just felt right.

Chase let him ramble on as his eyes drifted. He tried to keep up but he was getting more and more distracted by the radio and that God-awful music. Wallace saw this and stopped. The silence caused Chase to look up.

"Pennsylvania 6-5000"

"What?"

"The song title. Is it bothering you?"

Chase shrugged.

"I take it you don't like Glenn Miller."

"Never heard him before."

"No matter, I don't mind retuning the radio."
Wallace tried to tune in another station but was having a
hard time. "You know I built this myself."

"The radio?"

"Yup. I thought I should try to recreate all the great
invention before I started on my own."

Chase added from earlier, "Marconi's genius."

"Exactly. The transmission of sound through
wireless telegraphy. Based on electromagnetism."
Wallace tuned back in the big band/swing music. It was
back and still annoying to Chase.

"Does that have something to do with that Sakharov
guy?"

"Sahkarov definitely based his work on some of the
principles."

Chase got up. Something was rattling around in his
head. "I think you're giving me a hint."

Now Wallace was confused. "I'm what?"

"I think I know where you are!"

"Me? I'm right here."

"No! Not you, Wallace but you Wally."

"Wally? Who's Wally?"

"Is there a sun symbol in the house?"

"Sun symbol?"

"Yeah, one like this." Chase showed him the cover of the code book.

Wallace took the flashlight. He beamed it at the radio and then pointed it higher and higher until it shone over his bedroom window. It's a drawing...by Wallace....of the exact same symbol.

Chase opened the bedroom window and peeked out. There was a small landing outside of the window. It would protect his fall if this weren't the real portal. He felt good about that. He strapped his backpack over his shoulders. He lined himself up to take a running start at the opening. Before trying to leap through, he asked several things of Wallace: turn off the flashlight, look away (he didn't know why but thought the older Wally would require he say that), don't believe for a second that you're delusional and never stop working on your inventions. "And oh, there may be a lethal snake in your basement. Be careful when you go down there."

As Wallace pondered the snake in the basement, Chase ran and jumped from the second floor window. He didn't land on the roof of the farmhouse. He landed in a pile of dirt and grass. After pulling himself up from the side of the small mound he just face planted in, Chase looked for the first person he could find. He figured he just came through a small house window, so that's the first place he looked but nobody was in there. There were a few houses on the edge of the town so he ran to the next one and the next one. They were all empty. A young woman exited another house down the cobble-stoned street. Chase took off after her. He had one question.

Chapter 18

"Is this Bologna?"

Chase repeated himself, this time using his hands and much more animated. The young woman walking by was distracted but got it, "Bologna? Si."

Chase paused before a second question hit him. He fired away, "Signore Marconi?"

The woman pointed down the long arcade. She told him outside of town, there was a set of hills. She told him to walk into the countryside and he would see a crazy young man with metal and glass contraptions. That was Signore Marconi.

Chase did as he was told. As he left the city and journeyed into the grassy hills, he crested two hills and noticed a lanky young man in his twenties preoccupied with a metal and glass contraption. The man was halfway up the hill, a steep hill, that he looked to be climbing with purpose. He carried a wooden box with glass and metal components. Chase took off after him in a dead sprint.

"Signore Marconi?!" The man turned back to Chase. His face looked confused, like he wondered how this boy knew him. Still, he answered, "Si."

"Are you creating your genius?" As the words left his mouth, he realized this Italian man would not understand his question.

Then Marconi answered in fluent English, "My genius? What is my genius?"

Chase was more than stunned. "You know English!"

"Yes."

"How?"

"My mother is Irish." He stared at the boy. "Why does that matter?"

Chase shrugged.

Marconi remained focused on the boy. "What's my genius?"

Chase was about to say 'the radio' but then he caught himself. Marconi didn't know yet and Chase was not supposed to tell him. "I don't know. You tell me."

Marconi turned, annoyed with this little pest. He had work to do. Chase shouted another question that again stopped him in his tracks.

"Are you working on the wireless telegraphy thing?"

Marconi whipped his head around. "How did you know about that?"

The laser-like stare from Marconi caused Chase to take a step back. "I've...ah...just heard about you and what you're working on..."

Marconi had taken a few steps toward Chase and was now hovering over the boy. "I haven't shared any of this with anybody. So who told you about my work?"

"My grandfather. He's a big fan."

"Who's your grandfather? Tesla?"

Chase eked out, "Wally...Grandpa Wally."

"I don't know Wally or Grandpa Wally!"

"Well, he knows you."

Marconi studied Chase for a moment longer before storming off in a huff of cussing.

As he trekked back up the hill, the weight of all the boxes and metal sheets and pipes took its toll on the lanky man. He slipped, dropping one of the boxes. Chase watched for a moment as he fell again.

"May I help?"

Marconi, frustrated and now dirty, relented and waved the boy toward him.

Marconi had constructed his transmitter and receiver on the bottom of the hill. He told Chase that he was testing the radio over hills. Chase asked how far away the other person was. Marconi told him the receiver was over one kilometer away. He began to fire his machine up so he could send signals out into the air. From Chase's perspective, this contraption looked rather simple and clunky. That assessment earned another crusty look from Marconi.

Minutes later, Marconi began the experiment. He was again interrupted by Chase asking, "Where are the microphone and the speaker?"

Marconi was more than puzzled. Chase clarified. "Where are you going to speak into?"

"What?"

"And where do we hear the sound? The music?"

Marconi told him he was the most foolish young man he had ever run across. He said there would be no music. "The only music is the glorious sound of tapping on the coherer." Which was then explained to Chase to be a small glass tube filled with iron filings.

This prompted Chase to question Marconi's genius when it came to the radio, sending the scientist into a rage. To the outsider, Chase was not understanding the basic steps that had not yet been reached in the history of radio invention. The young time traveler was impatient when it came to watching and waiting on history to catch up to the future.

At the moment Marconi was about to banish Chase away, the receiver began tapping out the "Morse code" like message. Marconi stood statue-like. As he read the code, it was his distant partner confirming receipt of his message and respond in kind. Marconi began to jump around. He had successfully sent radio waves across a kilometer of land, hills and valleys, without the use of a wire. It was airborne communication.

And as quickly as they unpacked, Marconi…and Chase grabbed their gear and re-trekked the same hills. Chase followed Marconi back to the other transmission point. Earlier a pain in the rear, now Marconi utilized

Chase as a pack mule, carrying the tubes and antennae that were necessary for the experiment.

As they neared Marconi's house, two figures waited on the scientist. From a distance, Chase learned they were the operators of his other receiver and transmitter. One of these gentlemen was his professor and mentor, Augusto Righi from the University of Bologna. Chase asked who the other man was and Marconi did not know anymore than he was a friend of Righi and named Wallace.

"Wallace!?"

Marconi answered yes, but it was too late. The boy began a sprint toward the house. The two older men were chatting to each other when a scream interrupted their conversation.

"GRANDPA!"

Grandpa Wally turned around to see his young prodigy only twenty feet away and at a dead run. "Chaser! You made it!" The embrace Chase gave his grandfather was one of the greatest of history. He clamped on with as much passion and relief, several thousand years of time travel and history jumping could produce.

Grandpa Wally excused Chase and himself from any further duties with the 19th century scientists. He and Chase were going to walk back to Bologna and catch up on old times.

Out of earshot, Chase quizzed his Grandpa, "Do those guys know about the time?"

Grandpa answered quickly "Nope. Not at all."

"Were you here to see Marconi?"

"Sort of."

"Marconi's genius."

"Yeah, you saw the start of his success."

"That didn't look like a radio."

"It wasn't. He was just testing telegraphy. He needed to prove he could transmit over hills."

"And that helps you?"

"I have been here before and seen it. I was back to visit Signore Righi. He was the other man and Marconi's teacher."

"What did Righi invent?"

"It's not so much what he invented, as discovered and worked with."

Chase's face showed that Grandpa Wally should continue.

"Electromagnetism. He's an expert on electromagnetism. And that's what I'm more interested in at the moment."

Grandpa Wally leaned over and looked at his grandson.

"You look older."

"I do?"

"Yeah. You look older and different. Why is that?"

"I don't know. Maybe, it's because I've been through a lot."

Grandpa Wally nodded his head and chuckled at this young man in front of him. He had the look of pride and love.

"I was hoping you'd get my hints and get here as soon as possible."

"I got here as fast as I could but that was a lot of stops."

"Lot of stops?"

"Greece, Jersey, New York, London, Florence, Tuskegee, Tinkerton County and now here."

"What?! That wasn't the plan."

"Huh?" Chase was extremely confused. "What was the plan?"

"I wanted you to see ancient Greece and industrial America. Aristotle and Thomas Edison. Then Marconi."

"I did. And a whole lot more."

"Wait, did you say you went back home?"

"Sort of…"

Grandpa Wally's brow furrowed. "Back to the farm?"

"Yes…but it was 1956."

"'56! If you went back in '56 then you saw…"

"You. I saw you, Grandpa."

"You did?"

"You don't remember?"

Grandpa Wally stopped on the trail back to Bologna. He had to sit down and found a tree stump for that purpose. He looked deep in thought and that left Chase confused. Then a strange feeling came across Grandpa's face. He looked happy or maybe proud or maybe some weird combination of feeling good and bad and even boastful. Then Grandpa Wally looked distant. Chase would never wish ill on his Grandpa. He loved him too much. But after all the craziness he's just experienced, well it felt kinda good after all the chaos his Grandpa had just put him through. Chase took another look at Grandpa Wally and those thoughts disappeared. Now, Chase felt concerned.

"Are you OK, Grandpa?" Chase sat down next to him.

"Yeah."

"You don't look so hot."

Grandpa's head was shaking until a huge smile comes across his face. "I knew it! I knew I wasn't crazy!"

Chase became puzzled at the outburst. Grandpa noticed the confusion and began to explain. "I remember I had a horrible fever. And I remember I thought I was visited by some vision of this boy...who kinda looked like me. HA!"

"Chaser, come with me." Grandpa Wally jumped up from the tree stump and tore off down the road. "Man-oh-man, do I have some things to show you!"

They entered the city of Bologna in the late afternoon. The city buzzed as the pair walked through the arcades of the city. The covered sidewalks created a louder hum of shoppers and diners. Arched throughout, these structures hung out almost over the cobbled streets. Grandpa Wally was pointing out basilicas and museums, buildings and homes as they walked.

He seemed to have a purpose to his tour and they rolled up on the city university. He told Chase that Bologna was home to the oldest university in the Western world. "This is where higher education began.

The University of Bologna founded in 1088. This is where the word 'university' and 'alma mater' began!"

Grandpa grew more and more passionate as they walked through the campus streets. "Dante Alighieri studied here. So did Nicolaus Copernicus and Manuel Chrysoloras, Albrecht Durer, Luigi Galvani, Laura Bassi, even some of the members of the Medici family have connections at the university."

"Medici?"

"Yeah. They were a famous family. They were a very wealthy banking family but also great patrons to the arts. Hired painters like Michelangelo and da Vinci and Raphael. They are probably the most significant people that spurred the Italian Renaissance."

Chase was deep in thought as his Grandpa rambled on.

"What's so interesting about the Medici?"

"Nothing. Just heard the name before."

"Must have been when you were in Florence."

Chase agreed. "Yeah, must have been."

Grandpa Wally spotted something that took his voice even higher in excitement, "Are you hungry?"

"Yes!"

Grandpa Wally had found his favorite little Italian (of course) restaurant near the university.

"Most people would take you to a high brow restaurant down near the palazzo but this place is a hidden gem. You know Bologna is where Spaghetti Bolognese was created."

"Spaghetti Bolognese?"

"Spaghetti with meat sauce."

Chase smiled. He loved spaghetti with meat sauce.

After they ordered, Grandpa Wally was peppered with questions. These weren't about the sights of Bologna or any other place Chase had traveled. These questions focused on time travel and the system his grandfather had created...or found.

That became his Grandpa's first answer. "Created. But the principles were found in the great discoveries of past scientists."

"The portals had to be in the highest structures. Why?"

"Easiest for you to remember. And find. Just look up."

"Why the sun symbol?"

Grandpa Wally answered that with a question. "What's the one energy source that worked in ancient Greece all the way to present day?"

"The sun."

"Exactly. And each of the portals was solar powered. I mean, gosh golly, I put a sun on the door. It was truth in labeling."

It clicked for Chase. That made a lot of sense.

Chase inhaled the huge mound of pasta that was placed in front of him but managed to eke out another question through the spaghetti hanging from his mouth. "Grandpa, how do you control the time travel?"

"Your mind. You get to the next location when you're ready to move on."

"And getting back home?"

"You can only get back when your lesson is complete. When you've learned what you're supposed to learn. And not before."

"So it could take awhile."

"As short as it takes to learn or as long as you don't allow yourself to change."

"What if you don't want to learn? Or believe you'll change?"

"It's impossible not to experience these adventures and not change. But I have a rule: the cynical will not be transported. Belief is a must. Belief and a little fear."

"Fear?"

"Fear is in everything we do for the first time. It's merely an obstacle you overcome."

"Are you worried someone would find out about it and go back to change something in their life or make money some way?"

"This isn't just for the tourist in us. This isn't for the gambler to go back in time and make money for profit. I made sure of that when I designed it. I made sure it wouldn't work that way. The profit is in the lesson! The profit is in the adventure and the experience!"

"How do you control it?"

"First, by access. There are only two people in the world who know about this. And second, I'm working on the next level of security. How I can make it open to a few more people without it being opened to the world." Grandpa Wally stopped when he caught a glance of Chase's bowed head. "Chaser, what is it?"

"Nothing, Grandpa."

"No, Chaser, there is something on your mind. I know you way too well."

Chase knew his Grandpa would not let this go until he came clean.

"There aren't two…"

"What?!"

Chase hated to concede but he couldn't lie to Grandpa Wally. "There aren't two…"

"I thought I told you!"

"I did try. It was an accident!"

Grandpa Wally dropped his fork. He just lost his appetite. Then his head fell into his hands. He was going to need to hear all about Maddy. Chase sighed deeply and began.

When Chase finished, Grandpa Wally was conflicted. "That explains the additional stops."

"Huh?"

"The journey wasn't just yours. It was the journey of two thus you had additional adventures."

Chase thought that over. *If not for Maddy, he would have found Grandpa way earlier. Then again, if not for Maddy…he wouldn't have met a great friend and explored more of history.*

"That's why you found me once you left her."

"I'm sorry about her finding out."

"It's OK, Chaser. It doesn't sound like a mistake. So don't apologize. I think you are better for the experience."

Chase thought that over too.

"I'm not too happy about someone else knowing the ability to travel through time."

"She went back to the same year."

"And the same place?"

"Not exactly."

Chase explained that she went back to the same year but not the same location. Then Chase quickly added, "But she went to her grandfather's boyhood home. And she was working with a teacher named George at this black college."

"Black college?

"Yeah."

"In Alabama?

"Yeah."

"Teacher?

"Yeah."

"Could he have been a professor?"

"Yeah. I guess."

"Named George?"

"Yes."

"Wow. You met George Washington Carver?"

"I guess. He gave us some pretty lame peanut butter." Chase added, "She was going to stay and help him with his wagon."

"The Jesup wagon!"

"I guess. He was going to help the poor farmers with their crops. Get them off of cotton and on to peanuts."

"Chaser, you have to tell me more."

Chase went on to explain more of the adventures he had shared with Maddy. He told Grandpa Wally about flying with da Vinci and trying to save Jane Addams by attacking the figure they thought was Jack the Ripper. He told him about the racism that was in New York.

And he wondered why. New York wasn't racist in the 21st century.

His grandfather corrected him and said not as much but racism still existed everywhere. Chase accepted that idea because he knew his grandfather was right.

Then, he continued to tell more stories of their adventures. He told him about flying a hang glider and battling a snake and getting chased by Machiavelli and seeing the earliest of motion pictures. As he told his grandfather each and every story, he kept talking more and more about Maddy and how they worked together and how she pushed him when he got scared and how he helped her when she needed it.

"She sounds great. Sounds like you have a great friend." Grandpa Wally's words drifted off as he stopped talking and starting thinking.

"Grandpa, are you sure you're OK?"

"I was just thinking she sounded a little like your grandmother."

"Really?"

"Yeah. I know you never met her, but she was a special lady. Life hasn't been the same without her. The house hasn't been the same."

Chase chimed in. "Speaking of the house, can we go home? I loved this adventure but I'm tired and I miss Mom and Dad."

"Absolutely, Chaser. Let's head home!"

They left the restaurant, stuffed with loads and loads of pasta in their bellies. Grandpa Wally patted his belly in contentment and fulfillment, "I gotta tell you Chaser if there is one thing I've learned on these time travels is I sure do love Bologna."

Chase looked up at his Grandpa with a big smile. "What?"

Chase agreed, "Me too. I love Bologna too."

Grandpa motioned down the street, "Ready?"

"Absolutely."

They ventured down the tight streets of Bologna to the Torre Degli Asinelli. It was the larger of the two famous leaning towers of Bologna. Chase and Grandpa Wally gave one more look at the beautifully lit city before they strolled through the small back door of the tower and into a bright, white smoky setting.

A Billy club cut through the smoke and knocked Grandpa Wally off his feet. Chase turned, "Grandpa!"

Grandpa Wally had a hard time hearing Chase over the screeching police sirens, thunder of horses and barking dogs. Chase ran toward his Grandfather as a canister hit him in the side of the head. It began spewing tear gas.

"Chaser! Are you OK?!"

Chapter 19

"Chaser, are you OK?!?!"

"CHASER!"

"GRANDPA!"

They were standing four feet from each other and yet couldn't tell. The tear gas was too thick. And the chaos of the melee had turned them around.

WHOOSSHH! A policeman on horseback took a swing at Chase. He missed, coming within millimeters of his nose. Chase hit the ground and began to crawl to safety. Trouble is, he didn't know where that was.

Grandpa Wally had fallen backwards and fortunately so. He had found the curb and used it to feel his way from the smoke. When he came into a clearing, the scene became a little clearer. To his right, was a steel and concrete bowstring arch bridge and on the top of the structure he read its name: Edmund Pettus Bridge.

To Grandpa Wally's left, hundreds of people were being beaten by the police. Some on horseback, some on foot, all using some type of weapon: billy clubs, dogs or tear gas. They were beating an unarmed group of protestors, mostly African-American but some whites as well. He pushed back farther for a better view and perspective. Chase's location was his only goal.

He yelled for his grandson but those shouts were lost on the screams of those being beaten and those doing the beating. His eyes scanned the mess to no avail. As he was looking up, he didn't notice an older African-American woman lying on the ground. He tripped, almost landing on top of her. Gathering himself, he turned to apologize when he noticed she was bleeding profusely. Grandpa Wally went into action, whipping off his sweater and applying pressure to her shattered leg. He started yelling for help but the only people hearing him where others escaping the fracas and needing help themselves.

Inside the smoke, Chase crawled aimlessly. Instead of avoiding more action, he was heading straight into it. He realized this when he could feel the ground rising under him. He was crawling back up the incline of the bridge's roadway. The same direction the police were pushing many of the protestors that hadn't been injured. Chase realized higher ground would help his search so he rose and ran up the bridge a hundred feet or so. From that angle, he could see over and around the smoky blob that still held police and protestors. His eyed quickly scanned the mess until he spotted the white hair of Grandpa Wally. Off to the left and at the bridge landing, his grandfather huddled over a black woman. He was shielding her from any potential danger as best he could.

Chase's eyes then traveled back to the approaching fight. It was getting nearer and was blocking his pathway to his grandfather. After all this time travel, jumping and searching, obstacles and everything, he finally found his Grandpa and an hour later he might lose him again. Not this time!

Chase's acceptance of danger and risk had risen since his adventure began. He barely used one second to act. Sprinting straight ahead, the smoke enveloped Chase. His arms raised, Chase decided he'd give just as good as he got. A nightstick got close to him and instead of ducking, he waited until the swing paused and grabbed it. When he had hold of it, he yanked it. The policeman was caught off balance and nearly fell off his horse. With him out of control, Chase grabbed the reins and guided the horse to his left. He was shielding himself from most of the fighting and tear gas.

The horse got him through half of the mess. A couple of agile side steps and one duck between the horse's legs and he was even farther. But as lucky as Chase had been through most of the chaos, his luck turned quickly. For the second time that day, something hit him in the head. This was much more direct and much more painful than the tear gas canister. This was a nightstick to the back of the lower head. It was from the policeman he nearly pulled off the horse and it was a direct hit.

A blow to the back of the head, especially the lower part of it, right above the neck can cause a lot of damage.

In Chase's case, it caused him to lose his sight. The whole world went black. He was still awake but had no idea where he was, where he was going or what dangers might be nearby.

Chase was temporary blind. That was not in doubt. If he weren't blind, he would have surely seen the horse directly above him. And he would have shielded his face and head from that same horse that had risen up on its hind legs out of fear. It was spooked. And it was about to crush Chase.

That was until Grandpa Wally grabbed his arm and yanked him away. The only thing from that horse that hit Chase was the breeze of his whinny.

"Chaser. I got you."

"Grandpa?!" Chase still couldn't see and flailed his arms to feel where this voice was coming from.

"Chaser. Come on. Over here. We'll be safe."

Grandpa Wally led him out of the mess and back near the lady to which he was tending.

"Chaser, here, sit down. Sit down and catch your breath."

"Where Grandpa? I can't see."

Grandpa Wally guided Chase to the ground, leaning him against a large oak tree. He checked him as well as his amateur medical experience allowed him.

"Can you see at all?"

"Just a little light."

"Can you see shapes?"

"I'm starting to."

"OK, sit still. I see an ambulance over there. Wait right here!"

Grandpa Wally ran across the city block to the ambulances and began waving for them to follow. "Over here! I've got a young man who's been blinded and an elderly woman who's broken her leg."

One of the medics grabbed his bag and followed Grandpa Wally. When they arrived at his triage site, the medic stopped. "I'll look at the boy but I ain't helping no colored!"

"WHAT?! She's hurt."

"If I help her, I will be too."

"You jerk!" Grandpa Wally couldn't control himself and hauled back and punched his lights out.

"GRANDPA!"

Wally turned around to see Chase standing up. "Did you see that?"

Chase nodded.

A wave of calm came over Grandpa Wally, "Thank goodness." Then, a wave of regret and fear. He turned back to see the medic getting up and waving over the police for assistance.

"C'mon Chaser, grab this lady and let's get out of here!"

Chase and Grandpa Wally took the half dazed woman under each arm and proceeded to drag her away from the melee.

They quickly walk/ran down the city street searching for a safe spot to stop and regroup. They were slowed by the "almost" dead weight of the lady they were dragging. This getaway was not swift or easy. As they trudged to safety, their patient was falling in and out of consciousness.

"She's lost a lot of blood, Chaser. We have to get her to a hospital."

The woman's eyes had rolled back in her head. Then, she briefly popped back into reality. She was mumbling something.

Grandpa Wally was taller and thus his ear was farther away from her mouth. Chase, being shorter, could hear her more clearly.

"What's she saying?"

Chase leaned in. He then looked at his grandfather with a confused look. "She keeps repeating my name and saying Chase."

They continued running down the middle of the city street when a pedestrian stared in wonder at the sight of a white man and a white boy carrying a bleeding black woman.

Grandpa Wally seized on his attention. "She's lost a lot of blood. Where's the nearest hospital?!"

"For her?"

Grandpa Wally annoyingly nodded. "Yeah! Who else?!"

"For her, its across town."

"What do you mean across town?"

"The colored hospital is across town."

He pointed back over the river. "Over that bridge." The bridge that needed to be used was the bridge they were fleeing from in a hurry.

Grandpa Wally almost lost it again. The woman was getting worse and they were running out of energy.

"Oh Chaser…" Grandpa Wally was exasperated. "What do we have to do to get her some help?" Their speed has slowed even more. They were tiring. And that allowed the police to gain on their position.

Chase answered with the calm and reason of his 75 year-old grandfather. He confidently looked his grandfather in the eye and answered, "Jump."

Grandpa Wally paused for a second, agreed and looked around. So did Chase. The search for a portal began.

"Grandpa!" Chase was pointing to a small storefront in a five-story building. That's where they saw the prettiest vision they could have. The sign above it read: SUN TRAVEL AGENCY. Even better, the symbol above the door was that of a sun with sixteen rays coming out of the center. Eight were straight. Eight were squiggly.

Grandpa smiled. "I had forgotten…"

Their energy was restored as they ran full speed toward the plate glass window. There was no flinching, no hesitation and no fear. Three bodies crashed through the front of a small market in Selma, Alabama on March 7, 1965.

Three figures fell on the floor of the emergency room entrance seconds later. As the entire staff, families and patients whipped their heads to the door to see the commotion, Grandpa Wally yelled, "We have an emergency! This woman's in shock!"

Nurses and orderlies rushed toward them, scooping up the lady and hustling her into the ER. Grandpa Wally and Chase were in shock, too. But they were conscious and more stunned than shocked.

Each let out a huge sigh. Each heard the other. They looked each other over before hugging.

"Now that was an adventure!"

His Grandpa broke the embrace and began searching for information about their new location. Chase, however, winced. Something was poking him. He reached into his pocket and pulled out the small clipper ship. He smiled. It had made it through without being lost. He didn't have to burn this boat.

Grandpa Wally pointed to a sign in the ER lobby, "Good news, Chaser. The Mayo Clinic. Rochester, Minnesota. They'll save her."

"When?"

His Grandfather did a double take, "Now."

"No. When is it?"

Now his Grandpa understood. He grabbed a newspaper on the end table and read the top line. "April 4, 2010."

"WHAT!?"

"What?" his Grandpa wondered.

"That's the day after you disappeared."

"Meaning?"

"Meaning, that I went all over time and got back twelve hours later."

A nurse came out from the ER and yelled, "CHASE!"

"That's me!" Chase raised his hand.

"Your friend requested your presence."

Chase and Grandpa Wally wove through the chaos that was the emergency room and back to room three. When they entered, the elderly black woman looked at her two rescuers and smiled.

Chase asked a question, "Are you OK, ma'am?" He didn't expect the response he received. "Chase...?"

"Yeah?"

"Chasio?"

Chase's eyes popped open as wide as baseballs.

Chapter 20

"Chasio, is that you?"

Chase stared at her. "Maddy?"

"Chase!"

Chase didn't quite know what to say. He was a few days older. She was almost 70 years older. "How are you?"

"A little older, a little bigger but the same spirit as the twelve year-old girl you met long ago.

Chase still stammered over his words, "How'd you...? Why'd you...?"

Maddy calmed, "Chase, quiet."

Chase stopped immediately.

Then she got inquisitive. Her first question proved instantly to Chase that this was his old friend. "How long has it been since you've seen me?"

"Two days."

"Or sixty years." Both answers were correct depending on the person answering.

Chase went into his story. And how'd it had only been a few days. He explained Bologna and before that, seeing his grandfather as a boy.

That led to the introduction of Grandpa Wally and Maddy. Chase continued until his stories were done. Then, Grandpa Wally took over. He and Maddy talked like two old people who had known each other for years. They connected right away, were laughing and joking about things Chase saw no humor in.

At first, they teased Chase but then the conversation switched to the time machine and the science behind it. She peppered Grandpa Wally with questions and he answered each and every one. When he erased the white board in the room that listed her vitals and started lecturing, Chase ducked out.

Two hours later, Chase had grown tired of the waiting room television and dug into his backpack for the DS. It still had some juice left. Chase was surprised but then he thought it through. I really didn't play it that much...actually hardly at all. He fired up the game and waited for it to load.

As he did, his Grandpa interrupted him, "Are you playing that darn game?" Grandpa Wally had pushed Maddy into the waiting room in a wheelchair.

Chase shrugged, "I was about to...yeah...why?"

"Gee whiz Chaser, I sent you through the annals of time because of that game."

Chase didn't get the anger from Grandpa Wally. "Dude...this is the first time — !"

His grandfather did not hesitate, "Whatever adventure you're looking for isn't in that darn video game! Didn't you learn you just gotta go get it?"

"GRANDPA! I didn't play it all that much. Once but that's it. Look!" Chase held out the DS. "Look at the battery in the upper corner. It's practically full! And there was nowhere in ancient Greece or the Italian renaissance to plug-in."

Grandpa Wally lowered his head. He had unjustly jumped down Chase's throat. "I'm sorry Chaser, I said that without thinking." Grandpa Wally sat down next to Chase.

"You sent me on this because of a video game?"

Grandpa Wally nodded. "Among other things." Grandpa paused to chuckle to himself, "Every time I'd hear from your mother, she'd tell me you had your nose stuck in that game. And she said you were telling her that school was getting more and more boring. And I was getting upset."

"About me playing video games?!"

"Yeah!" Grandpa shouted a little too loud and a little too quickly. The entire waiting room turned to look at the hubbub. They both start laughing at Grandpa's excitement. They headed back to Maddy's room.

"Seriously Chaser, I am sorry. I didn't mean to accuse you of something that you didn't do. And I wanted to say how proud I am of you. You went farther and further than I imagined. You handled yourself like a young man, not a timid boy. It's really impressive. I wish I could have seen you in action."

"Well, maybe we can do it again."

"Really? You'd jump again?" Grandpa Wally inquired.

"Yeah...I mean not tomorrow but, yeah."

"No. Not tomorrow. Tomorrow, _we_ head back to the farm."

Chase smiled bigger than he ever had.

Grandpa turned to Maddy, "Would you like to see my farm?"

Maddy didn't answer. She was fixed on the television. The newscaster was talking about some story about some bill moving through Congress. But it wasn't the bill that glued her eyes. It was when the newscaster mentioned the opinions of the White House and the President. She was staring at video of Barack Obama.

"The President of the United States is black?"

They both nodded. It wasn't big news to them. It _was_ to a woman who nearly died marching for the right to vote only a few hours ago.

Last time Chase headed to the farm, the car ride was quiet. Quiet and sad. Not this time. Chase, Maddy and Grandpa Wally were laughing and joking.

The excitement of rounding the roadway and creeping up the last hill near a grove of oaks and pines swept over the group. The spires of the house pierced the sky. A few more seconds and the entire house would come into view. And when they rounded the hill, the farmhouse stood atop the horizon like it always had for the past hundred years. And it didn't look lonely and decrepit. Now, it looked warm and inviting.

When Chase's parents asked about their whereabouts, Grandpa Wally explained they were at the hospital with his friend and there was no need to worry.

"And where have you been all morning, Chaser?"

"All morning?"

"Yeah. When your father and I woke up, we looked all around for you."

"Just this morning?"

"Yes, just this morning. We knew where you were last night. Where were you this morning?"

"Out...looking for Grandpa."

"Where?"

"Just around."

Later, Chase was staring out the window of his farmhouse bedroom. The same window he had jumped from fifty-four years earlier. There was no sun symbol above it but the same barn and lawn.

"You're not thinking about jumping, are you?

Chase turned around to see Grandpa Wally.

"No. Just thinking."

"About the travels?"

"Yeah...and that it all happened because I play video games?"

Grandpa chuckled. "All that because life is worth living." Chase didn't quite understand. "You can't tell me you didn't have a blast."

Chase rolled his eyes.

"And you can't tell me you've gotten more excitement from those games?"

"So that's what you wanted to teach me?"

"Yeah. I guess…in a roundabout way." Grandpa Wally sat down on the bed. "Chaser, life is always there to teach you something. And no matter who you are, you've got something to learn. Now, I'm not talking about facts and figures or math and history. I'm talking about big lessons. You understand?"

"Not really."

"When I was a boy, nothing ever came to me fast enough. I couldn't grow up fast enough. I couldn't wait to drive a car fast enough. I couldn't graduate from high school fast enough. Nothing was fast enough. But slowly, after being frustrated and getting angry and learning that the world worked on its own schedule, I overcame that. Now I take things a lot easier. For you, I could tell you were a boy that was growing up and not attacking the world but rather letting it attack you. You'd retreat into those games because it was easier to conquer them than the real world. I know about school. And your friends. And how you're shy. And a little scared to try new things. Like athletics or clubs or groups. I know you're smart, but you disengage in certain classes. Like history. But I know you can do anything if you put your mind to it. So instead of you putting your mind to it, I gave you a little nudge."

"Little?"

"When you let fear dictate the terms, you'll always lose that negotiation. When you attack fear, it doesn't seem so scary."

Grandpa patted him on the shoulder, "And that's the lesson for this adventure."

"So what's the next lesson I'm going to learn?"

"I don't know yet. But you'll find it on your own. And you'll recognize it in due time."

"So what's yours then?" Chase added. "You said even you have lessons to learn."

"Well, I've been moping and feeling sorry for myself for the past ten years since your Grandma passed away. And I've been real lonely. But I think that might change after the past few days."

The next morning Chase asked again, "You sure, Maddy?"

As they day wound down, the Axelrod family had packed up the car, ready to head back to New York City, but before they could travel the roads back to Minneapolis and the airport, Chase felt compelled to visit the guest room to say goodbye to his friend.

"Yeah. I'm going to stay with your Grandpa Wally for a while. I don't know how many days I have left on this planet and I'm interested in seeing as much of it <u>and</u> its past, as I can."

Chase got it. Maybe at 75, he'd feel the same way. Plus, he figured he'd cross path with her again.

"I, now, see why you were so adamant to find this man." Chase turned to look over his shoulder. His Grandfather stood in the doorway.

Chase teased back, "Yeah…I guess. I'm sorta regretting the whole trip, the more I think about it."

Chase and his parents couldn't get back to New York and their own beds fast enough. Chase knew that from the conversation his parents had in the car, on the plane and in the cab. It was hard, but Chase bit his tongue. They had been away from home for two days. He had traveled the world and all of time. His yearning was a little bit stronger.

Chase lay in bed as a rush of memories hit him. His brain downloaded and an entire movie played in his head. And he loved it. His eyes darted around the room. All the mementos that his grandfather gave him lined the shelves and walls. Some triggered old memories. Some triggered new adventures. He didn't want it to end, even as his eyelids grew heavier and heavier. He was quickly falling asleep.

When the daylight crept in the window, Chase fought it as hard as he could. He rolled over time and time again but whether it was the sunlight, the buzz of New York City, the smell of pancakes coming from under the door or the fact that it was Monday and a school day, Chase finally stopped fighting it.

He was about to get out of bed when he noticed something hanging over his bedroom door. It was a sun symbol, just like the drawing Grandpa Wally had over the window in his room back in 1956. He stared at it for a moment before getting on with his day.

Chase got dressed and grabbed some of his things, shoving them in his backpack. He looked up at the sun symbol again. He paused. He placed his hand on the doorknob but didn't turn it. A thought went through his head. Nope, not again. Not yet. I'm tired and I've got school. Besides, he's just going to go to the bathroom to brush his teeth and head downstairs.

He turned the doorknob and stepped into the hallway.

Except...he didn't make it to the bathroom. Nope. And he's wasn't in New York anymore.

Now, he stood in the middle of the thick forest. On the side of a mountain. With all the trees and leaves, it made it dark. Chase Axelrod looked in front of him. Trees surrounded the small mountain shack from which he just stumbled out of. Behind him: No cabin but more trees. Lots and lots of trees...and when he squinted...and looked down the hill. Something was moving. He squinted. It moved. He focused. It kept running. Toward him.

It was a bear. Big. Hairy. Snarling.

It looked hungry. And it wasn't stopping.

"GRANDPA!!!!!!!!"

APPENDIX

A chapter-by-chapter historical
study guide for the novel.

CHAPTER 1

Guglielmo Marconi
Nikola Tesla
Electromagnetic waves
The radio
Latin and Greek
languages

CHAPTER 2

Romans
Visigoths
Trojans
Spartans
Normans
Saxons

CHAPTER 3

Minnesota
Hernando Cortes
Clipper ships

CHAPTER 4

Ancient Greece
Mastic
Tunic
Thebes
Aristotle

CHAPTER 5

Corinthian War
Leuctra/Thebes
Peloponnesian War
Peloponnesian League
Democracy
Oligarchy

CHAPTER 6

Plato
The Parthenon
Athens
Pericles
Athena
Ancient City-States

CHAPTER 7

Film Projection
The Light Bulb
Stock Ticker
Thomas Edison
Menlo Park
Glenmont

WANT MORE CHASE?

Games, Puzzles, Trivia and more!

All available for downloading.

Please visit
www.chasethroughtime.com
to download.

Passcode: BACKPACK